Fürst und Bolf

Missionary Voyages among the South Sea Islands

Fürst und Bolf

Missionary Voyages among the South Sea Islands

Inktank publishing, 2018

www.inktank-publishing.com

ISBN/EAN: 9783747781029

MISSIONARY VOYAGES

AMONG THE

SOUTH SEA ISLANDS.

WITH ENGRAVINGS FROM ORIGINAL DESIGNS.

BOSTON:

PUBLISHED BY CLAPP & BROADERS.

1834.

ADVERTISEMENT.

The materials of this volume have been furnished by the attractive Voyages of the ship Duff, of Jefferson, W. Ellis, Stewart, and others, among the Islands of the South Sea. These Voyages are interesting from the novel and striking incidents in which they abound, independently of the importance they derive from the great purposes which prompted them.

As there is no subject of a nature to excite more lively interest than the diffusion of religious truth, there is none to which the attention of the young should be more early called.

We believe the tendency of the present volume will be to excite their sympathies, and make them aware of their duty, in imparting the blessings of Christianity to those beautiful islands where nature has so lavishly scattered her bounties.

CONTENTS.

CHAPTER XIII.

CHAPTER XIV.

MISSIONARY VOYAGES.

CHAPTER I.

Interest excited in England for the South Sea islanders by the narratives of Captain Cook and other navigators. Formation of the Missionary Society. Sailing of the Duff, and occurrences of the voyage. Arrival at Rio Janeiro. First sight of the South Sea islands. Arrival at Otaheite, or Tahiti.

THE attention of Europe was first drawn to the fertile and delightful islands of the South Sea, by the narratives of the various navigators, sent out on expeditions of discovery by order of George the Third, king of England. The interesting accounts of the voyages of Captain Cook, and the adventures he met with among the simple islanders, are read with much eagerness by all classes. To the Christian portion of the community, a new field offered itself for the diffusion of religious truth. An association was formed in

2

London in September 1795, under the name of the Missionary Society, with the view of attempting to spread the blessings of the gospel among the indolent yet generous people, who inhabited these romantic regions.

This plan was favoured by a number of happy circumstances. It was no great hardship to leave the northern and foggy climate of Great Britain, for the healthful and delicious airs of a southern sky. Every day added new proof, from new adventurers, of the beauty of these islands, the richness of their soil, and their luxurious productions. The character of the natives was also highly interesting; they were simple in their feelings, graceful in their forms, abundantly provided by nature with the necessaries of life, and ready to share them with strangers.

The formation of the Missionary Society was considered as the commencement of a new era, in the history of religion and of man. Sermons were every where preached, and meetings held throughout the kingdom. Funds poured in from all quarters for the promotion of the Society's popular undertaking: for the intelligent of the

British public soon became interested in the project, and ready to extend to it all the assistance in their power.

Under such favourable circumstances, it was not long before the members of the newly formed society found themselves zealously seconded in every way. Numerous candidates soon appeared, eager to exile themselves from all that was dear in Europe, and to engage in the civilization and conversion of the islanders in this remote region of the globe.

At length, a committee of ministers selected from among the applicants a company of thirty men, who, with the wives of six of them, and three children, were presented to the directors, to form the first colony, as a commencement of the mission. Of these persons, four were ordained ministers. One was a surgeon; the remainder of them were artisans of different descriptions, and all considered to be animated by the spirit proper for their important undertaking. The ship was placed under the care of Captain James Wilson, a commander every way qualified for so responsible a charge.

On the tenth of August, 1796, the Duff weighed anchor in the morning, and hoisting the missionary flag, sailed down the Thames, amidst the cheers and blessings of hundreds, animated by the same spirit with those who were parting forever from their native homes. The struggles of a last separation with friends and relations were over; distant seas and foreign shores were now the objects of anticipation to all. They commended themselves to the guidance and protection of Him, who has the winds of heaven at his command; and thus this religious company, worshipping as they went, sailed from the Downs, 'with songs of rejoicing.'

The voyagers had pleasant weather, and on the eleventh of October, their ship crossed the tropic of Cancer. All on board being by this time well recovered from sea-sickness, the flying fish, and other novelties of a tropical sea, over which they were now making rapid way, excited 'much surprise and admiration.' On the fourteenth they touched at St. Jago, one of the Cape de Verd islands, and sailing thence, they, on the twelfth of November, cast anchor

ENTRANCE TO RIO-JANEIRO.

Page 11.

under the white walls of the Benedictine monastery in the harbour of Rio de Janeiro.

'On entering the port, after a long passage across the Atlantic,' says their Journal, 'the vastness of the prospect fills the mind with the most pleasing sensations.' Passing the narrow entrance between two lofty hills, the harbour, suddenly widening, shews like an extensive lake, with many islands fancifully scattered on its bosom. The white-washed walls of the city, shining in the sun at the bottom of the harbour, with the lofty fortifications frowning over it, and the numerous boats among the shipping, presented a scene which deeply struck the missionaries.

'Beyond all,' they continue, 'to the northwest, as far as the eye can reach, a range of lofty mountains erect their rugged tops; in their bosoms, perhaps, thousands of human beings are doomed, in search of gold and diamonds for avaricious masters, to spend their days in unrelieved misery. On approaching the harbour, the tops of the mountains were hid in clouds, but the hills near the shore were covered with fruit trees to their very tops. Several fortified islands were around us, and on the main we saw a magnificent aqueduct of about fifty arches, extending from one mountain to another.'

The English strangers were greatly struck with the beauty of the viceroy's garden, and the view of the harbour from one of the terraces of the palace; as well as, by contrast, with a scene disgusting to humanity, the exposure of a cargo of human beings, naked in the market-place. This was in 1796, when Rio was entirely possessed by Portugese, natives, and slaves.

The number of priests whom they met was immense. The shops with which the streets were filled, particularly those of the druggists and silversmiths, made a very noble appearance, but the number of saints at every corner, to which the inhabitants were constantly kneeling and crossing themselves, as on many parts of the continent, made the missionaries exclaim, that the people seemed to be utterly sunk in idolatry.

On the twentieth of the same month, the Duff again set sail from Rio, having taken in such provisions there as the place afforded. Proceeding south towards Cape Horn, they found the atmosphere free from clouds both by day and night, the breezes moderate, and the weather mild. But on the night of the twenty-ninth, the terrified missionaries were roused from their sleep by the noise of the elements, and crowding on deck found their ship under bare poles, the sea running mountains high, and the heavens sending forth heavy flashes of lightning. The threatened tempest, however, partly moderated; but after a few days, finding the weather colder as they proceeded towards the south, and becoming apprehensive of danger, in the attempt to double Cape Horn, Captain Wilson changed his plan, and determined on altering his course for the passage to the South Sea by the east.

Standing, therefore, on this new course, he passed the Cape of Good Hope, a few degrees to the south, on the twenty-fourth of December; intending to keep to the south of New Holland and New Zealand, and then, on getting into the tract of the trade winds, to steer northerly for Otaheite, or more correctly Tahiti.

During this long voyage, the missionaries employed themselves in the study of the Tahitian language, and the details of the geography of those islands, among which they expected to spend the remainder of their lives. Medicine also formed part of their studies, under the instruction of Mr. Gilham their surgeon, who delivered to them lectures upon a prepared human skeleton ; and such as chose it learned from each other, the several handicrafts of which they were master. On board, the Sunday was always kept in the strictest manner, as it would have been on shore, the missionaries preaching alternately. On the twenty-ninth of December, they observed an eclipse of the sun that lasted for three hours, in the course of which about two thirds of the great luminary were obscured.

At seven in the morning of the twenty-second of February, a seaman on the fore-yard arm, set up the welcome shout of land. This proved to be the island of Tabouai, then above twenty-five miles off; but the wind having shifted, it was near evening when they found themselves nearly in shore, the sea breaking violently upon the reefs of rock which surrounded the island. Through the dusk of the evening, the anxious ship's company could see a border of low land running down from the hills towards the sea, from which the tall stems of cocoa-nut trees shot up abundantly between them and the sky. But a sight of the land was all that the missionaries at this time obtained, for the majority of them having determined on settling at Tahiti, the ship stood away during the night for the latter island, which was still some days' sail from them.

On the morning of Saturday, March the fourth, after a stormy passage from Tabouai, the missionaries beheld at a great distance through the clear atmosphere, the long wished for island of Tahiti. During the whole of the day, however, the variable wind obliged them to stand off and on, between its lesser peninsula and the neighbouring island of Eimeo. Passing the Saturday night off the land, occupied with many conflicting emotions, on Sunday morning, the fifth of March, by seven o'clock, the missionaries found themselves wafted by a gentle breeze, close upon the romantic shores of the island for which they were destined, and already saw numerous canoes filled with natives, putting off and paddling for the ship.

CHAPTER II.

Canoes of the natives surround the Duff. Anecdotes. Sunday on board ship. The Matilda. Priest Haamanemane. Missionaries land at Matavai Bay. Astonishment of the natives. Anecdotes of the King and Queen. Matavai ceded to the Missionaries. Tea drinking. Anecdotes. Appointment of preachers.

The Duff had no sooner drawn near to the shore of Tahiti, than the missionaries could count not less than seventy-four canoes filled with natives, already swarming round the ship. Captain Wilson tried to keep the islanders from crowding on board, but in spite of all his efforts, there were, in a few minutes, above an hundred of them on deck, dancing and capering, and crying "Taio! taio!" (their word for friend,) mixed with a few English terms, which had been taught them by former visitors.

The joyous Tahitians had neither weapons of

war of any sort in their hands, nor much that could be called dress upon their persons. But the missionaries were disappointed in their appearance, and became distrustful from their wild and disorderly behaviour. Their cheerfulness, good nature, and generosity, however, soon removed all unfavourable impressions.

It is a custom with these simple people, to select from among such strangers as visit them, one to whom they attach themselves as a Taio, or friend, with whom they interchange presents and kindnesses. An aged priest named Haamanemane, much distinguished among the natives, was very desirous to become Taio with the captain, as were others of the strangers to be on the same terms with the officers of the ship; but as the nature of this engagement was as yet very imperfectly understood by the Englishmen, they, for the present, declined this sudden friendship, to the great surprise of the generous natives.

The astonishment of the islanders was much increased, when the Europeans next declined the offers of hogs, fowls, and fruit, which they brought to them in abundance. This was for a reason which the missionaries tried in vain to make them understand, namely, because the day (Sunday) being devoted to God, [Eatua,] they, the Christians, were forbidden to transact any matter of business or barter. As the extravagant joy and generosity of the natives gradually subsided, many left the ship, and others were driven away by the old priest, who seemed to have much authority among them. About forty still remained, who being brought to order, the missionaries proposed, as the day was Sunday, to have divine service on deck in presence of the barbarians.

During sermon and prayers, the wondering strangers were quiet and thoughtful, but when the singing of the hymns commenced, their delight and amazement knew no bounds. Sometimes they would talk and laugh while worship was going on, but a slight sign or nod of the head again brought them to quietness and order, and that in a degree which, justly excited the surprise of the missionaries.

A ship called the Matilda having been lost in these seas about five years before, and accounts having reached England that some of her crew had found an asylum in Tahiti, the missionaries made such inquiries as they could concerning these men, in the hope, that should any of them be yet on the island, they might prove exceedingly useful to the new colonists. The answers of the people were very unsatisfactory, but the news of the arrival of a British ship having quickly spread over the island, those on board soon saw two men different from the natives, though tattooed about the arms and legs, and wearing part of the Tahitian dress, coming in a canoe by themselves towards the ship.

Coming on board they proved to be Swedes; the youngest, about thirty, had been one of the crew of the Matilda; and the other named Peter Haggerstein, aged forty, had been left on the island by the Captain of the Dœdalus. These men were tolerably versed in the general history of the island, spoke pretty good English, and having become well acquainted with the Tahitian tongue, the missionaries considered their presence, and promised assistance, very favourable omens.

It appeared, from the account of the Swedes, that the old priest Haamanemene was a person of very great consequence, having formerly been king of one of the neighbouring islands. This induced the Captain to treat him with more respect, so he invited him into the cabin, and treated him with the distinction to which kings and arch priests think themselves entitled. On the following morning he consented to become his taio, and they exchanged names, as was the custom of the islanders in the performance of that ceremony.

Haamanemane wrapped a piece of cloth round his new taio, put a teboota over his head, and then made him understand that the present of a musket with some gunpowder and shot, would be very acceptable, to cement all this friendship. But the Captain, having signified that it was not convenient at present to gratify him in this particular, the good natured old priest was satisfied with a promise of re-payment for all friendly services hereafter to be performed.

On the afternoon of this day, Monday, the sixth of March, the Duff having drawn nearer to the shore within a beautiful harbour, called Matavai Bay, prepared for landing most of the missionaries on the following morning. In the mean time, Haamanemane having departed to prepare the king for their reception, not only did so, but coming again on board early in the morning of the seventh, brought with him to his taio, the captain, a present of hogs, fowls, bread-fruit, cocoanuts, and even a quantity of cloth manufactured by the natives.

About eleven in the forenoon, the weather being fine, the missionaries and their wives prepared to land. Hundreds of natives now crowded on the beach, and as the ship's boats drew near, many of the delighted islanders rushed into the water, and hauling them aground, took the Captain and the others on their backs and carried them dry to the shore. Here the strangers were received by the young King and his Queen, who had been waiting for their landing; and taking Captain Wilson and the missionaries by the hand, they surveyed them for a time in dumb curiosity. But the clearness of the skins of the fair Europeans, appeared principally to attract the attention of the Queen, and fill her with astonishment. Yet this was nothing to the effect produced by the European women and children (such having never before been seen in the South Seas) upon the amazed natives; who now also, as when they saw them on board the ship, set up a cry of delight and astonishment.

The name of the king was Otu, and his wife Tetua. They were both handsome, and well proportioned in their persons, particularly the queen, and neither was more than seventeen years of age. Otu afterwards received the title of Pomare the Second, a name remarkable in the history of Tahiti and of missions. The pride of birth, and rank, is very great among these islanders; and the persons of the king and queen are so respected, that they are carried on men's shoulders, because, wherever they set their feet, the spot is considered sacred, and in some sense, to be used only by themselves. Yet this royal state is but little consistent with some of the practices of these august personages, for the missionaries observed, that upon occasions when the king and queen came off to the Duff in their canoes, her majesty made herself very useful, by baling out the water with a cocoa-nut shell.

The reception of the missionaries in the island of Tahiti was altogether most flattering. They were officially welcomed by an old chief, named Paitia, and a large house at hand, which had been built by Pomare for Captain Bligh, a former visitor, whom he expected to return to the island, was in the mean time offered for their immediate accommodation. This house was most agreeably situated on a long flat neck of land, which forms the northern boundary of Matavai Bay, and which sweeps by a delightful river.

It was on this spot that, many years before, Captain Cook had erected tents, and fixed his instruments, for the purpose of making some astronomical observations. Point Venus afterwards became the name by which it was distinguished. Backed by lofty mountains of the most romantic forms, and surrounded by groves of the picturesque trees of these regions, this must have been a charming spot. When the missionaries had taken possession of this building, and fitted it up for their accommodation, with gardens and outhouses; impressed by present appearances, they exclaimed, 'Thus hath the

Lord set before us an open door, which we trust none shall henceforth be able to shut.'

The next thing the generous islanders did for the missionaries, besides supplying them, in abundance, with all sorts of their native provisions, was to cede to them formally, not only the house originally intended for Captain Bligh, but the whole district of Matavai, in the neighbourhood.

This singular transaction, so much resembling the solemn treaties of Penn with the chiefs of the aboriginal Americans, took place in the open air, in the presence of the king and queen, the chiefs, and high priest of the island, and of Captain Wilson and all the missionaries, with their wives and children. A transaction so important to the cause of religion and philanthropy; a contrast so striking between wild barbarism and thoughtful civilization, as such a meeting held among the romantic valleys of an island of the South Sea, must have exhibited,—makes this treaty between the naked Tahitians and the sober missionaries ever memorable.

The first few weeks after their arrival was, by the new settlers, chiefly taken up in exchanging acts of kindness with the natives, preparing their new habitations, and other arrangements for their permanent comfort. They found a good friend in the old high priest, Haamanemane, who was the principal actor in the ceremony of conveying the land to them. For this and other favours, the Captain made him a present of a metal watch, with which the old man was delighted. The management of a watch being, however, a charge for which his talents were as yet inadequate, Peter, one of the Swedes, formerly mentioned, was directed to wind it up daily for its new owner.

Pomare and his wife went on board the Duff, as did also the old priest; being invited into the cabin, they showed an excellent relish for English living, drinking tea and delighting in wine, as if they had been accustomed all their lives to these luxuries. The manner in which Pomare drank his tea is somewhat amusing. His dignity not allowing him to feed himself, an attendant, having poured the tea from the cup into the saucer, held the latter to his mouth, and thus he swallowed his tea, as well as his other victuals.

But in this manner he contrived to devour such quantities of victuals, that the missionaries were astonished; for, at his first supper, he ate a whole fowl, with the addition of about two pounds of pork, and drank in proportion.

On one occasion, when the old priest was on board, king Otu and his queen, not being disposed to go to the ship, sent their presents only, and expressed a wish to see one of the great guns fired. This being consented to, and two of the guns being unloosed, the priest desired to have the honour of firing them off.

Although almost blind, he took the match and applied it with the greatest readiness; and having performed this feat, he was quite transported at his own unexpected courage. In the evening, when Pomare and he had eaten and drank freely, the latter began to inquire for amusements; first, for the letting off of sky-rockets, as former captains had done; next, for a violin and dancing. Finding himself disappointed in all these, taking a roll of cloth under his arm, and twisting his body in a humorous position, like a Highland piper, he seemed to inquire for the gratification of a tune upon that melodious instrument, the bagpipe. When the chief found that even this piece of amusement was wanting in the ship, he was by no means pleased; and when some one treated him with a spring upon the German flute, he did not seem quite satisfied with so delicate a species of music.

On their voyage, before their arrival, the missionaries had agreed, conformably to the wishes of their friends in England, to make Tahiti the head quarters of the Mission, yet to divide themselves, if possible, throughout the three groups of the neighbouring islands. Four ministers, with their wives and families, were to remain at Tahiti, and, the colony being now pretty well settled, the twelve remaining missionaries, with Captain Wilson, prepared for their departure; and it being deemed necessary to set apart two of their number, especially for the office of preachers, Sunday, the nineteenth of the present month, March, was appointed for the purpose.

The missionaries describe this solemnity as peculiarly pleasing to their own feelings, and interesting from the external circumstances. It having been given out among the natives, that on the next day of God (Sunday) their new friends intended to address them, numbers gathered early in the morning round their dwelling, amongst whom was the chief Pomare with his sister, who said that 'he had been dreaming about the book which should be sent him from the Eatua.' At ten in the morning, the straggling natives were called together from their indolent idling in the neighbouring groves and valleys.

A multitude was soon assembled under the shade of some large and lofty trees, and near to the stream which wound down from the mountains. Seats were placed for the chief and his sister, while the rest of the natives stood in a circle around. The missionaries sat close under the trees, their appearance strongly contrasting with the naked simplicity of the islanders, as on the day of the former great meeting when the conveyance of the land took place. The spectacle could not have been otherwise than affecting to the humane and the religious. 'God so loved the world,' was the text of the missionary who addressed the islanders, 'that he gave his only Son, that they who believe might not perish, but have everlasting life.' His first preaching in this romantic part of the island, must have been, according to the picturesque expression of the Baptist, like a voice crying in the wilderness. 'The Tahitians,' say the missionaries, 'were silent and solemnly attentive,' although every sentence of the preacher required to be repeated by the interpreter; and when the whole was over, the chief, taking the preacher by the hand, said, 'there were no such things before in Tahiti.'

Nor was the remainder of the service of the missionaries, among themselves on that day, less solemn and affecting. The laying on of hands upon two of their number, ordaining them to the same avocation in distant islands, to which they were now about to depart, together with the accompanying charges and responses, was a touching ceremony in these remote regions. Yet, though far distant from that country in which their own God was 'well known,' they knew that on that day, being Sabbath, thousands of prayers were offered up for their success; and, though like the children of the captivity, they sang their song in a strange land, they were not without that fellowship which the spirit can enjoy. The sacrament of the union, of which they all partook, added greatly to the solemnity, and the bread-fruit of Tahiti was used for the first time, as a symbol and memorial of the great event of the Christian faith.

On the second day after this, before daylight in the morning, the Duff, with the remaining missionaries, weighed anchor, and sailed from the island of Tahiti.

CHAPTER III.

The Duff arrives at Eimeo. The harbour and inhabitants of this island described. Departure of the Duff. Palmerston's Island. Arrival at Tongatabu. Two Englishmen found on the island. Landing of the missionaries. Visit of a tall chief, and of a corpulent lady of rank. Departure of the Duff.

SAILING from Matavai Bay in Tahiti, amidst a fresh gale with thunder and lightning, the Duff was in a few hours off the north east side of the neighbouring island of Eimeo, the weather having by this time become moderate. Running along the edge of coral reefs into Taloo harbour, they cast anchor quite near to a remarkably large tree, which grew close to the water's edge. The mouth of this harbour is about a quarter of a mile broad, and the sea is of wonderful depth; yet is the water so perfectly clear, that a little within the beautiful bay, the bottom can be distinctly seen; the coral in the most fantastic forms, branching along and upwards in the crystal element.

This romantic bay struck the missionaries as an exceedingly interesting spot. Its deep solitude and silence had something awful in it, notwithstanding its beauty, for it is so perfectly land-locked, that not a ripple of water appears on the shore. It is bordered with trees growing down to the very beach, from the surrounding hills. A fresh water river, of navigable depth, run several miles inwards among the mountains: a tree resembling the lignumvitæ mixed with the lofty cocoa nut on the hills, and wholly covered a single small island, which, like the haunted fairy islands of romance, stood solitary in the bosom of these glassy waters.

Amidst the solitudes which surrounded this noble bay, the missionaries saw, for the first time in these regions, a native burying-place; and afterwards several canoes, filled with the islanders, broke the still waters of the bay, and were seen to draw towards the ship. When the natives came on board, the Captain offering to barter with them for provisions, he found they had brought no hogs with their other articles, by which he first became acquainted with a singular custom. So many of these animals are occasionally destroyed by the islanders, in their feastings, or during the ceremonies of their barbarous idolatry, that the chiefs find it necessary for the prevention of famine, to prohibit the eating or selling of their most necessary provision, which extends often to the very fish of the surrounding sea. The missionaries, however, felt no inconvenience from this law, having been plentifully supplied before their departure from Tahiti, by their generous native friends in Matavai bay.

A number of canoes, filled with men and women, had paddled about the Duff, a great part of the day; and a considerable number of the natives, some with only a log of wood to hold by occasionally, and others without any thing whatever, swam about and diverted themselves in the sea around, with the carelessness and ease of water-fowls in a pond. The sailors in the ship would sometimes throw them a trinket or some other small article, and though the depth of the sea was unknown to the islanders, they would dive after it, and seldom fail to bring it up again. Still the manner and aspect of these people indidicated to Captain Wilson a disposition to thievishness, which caused him to watch closely such as he admitted on board.

During the same night, it being very dark, the deck watch observed a naked native standing alone in the main chains, without the bulwarks of the ship. The man who first saw the islander instantly attempted to seize him where he stood, upon which he jumped into the sea and disappeared: but when he was gone it was found that he had taken away about four yards of the electric chain, which hung outside for the protection of the ship.

On the twenty fourth, while the Duff still lay in Toloo harbour, in the middle of the day, as the Captain and missionaries were at dinner in the cabin, a canoe came quietly under the ship's stern, and a tall native, climbing up on the back of the rudder, got close to the cabin windows, and reaching in his hand, snatched up a book, the only article near; with which, he sprang backwards, and plunged into the water. Upon hearing this, all those, who sat at the table started up, and getting upon deck, pursued the offender.

The man, however, for a long time eluded the pursuit of the sailors, with the dexterity of a wild duck; but with the assistance of their pinnace, and by frightening him with firing small shot, they at last caught him. The poor savage trembled much and struggled hard; but a rope having been bound round his body, he was hoisted on board the ship, and then lashed to the rigging for a warning to his countrymen, who stood round the beach to witness his punishment.

Having exposed him thus for a time, Peter, the Swede, was desired to inform him in what light the Captain considered his offence, and simply warning him and his countrymen against the repetition of similar depredations, the trembling islander was released, to the great joy of himself and his people.

Captain Wilson and his friends found the natives of Eimeo far behind the Tahitians in every species of approach towards civilization; and so thievishly inclined, that they even stole the rudder out of the jolly-boat that lay alongside the ship. But little was known by the missionaries, however, regarding the people of this island; for

Captain Cook having long before inflicted severe vengeance on them for stealing his goats, the new visitors were unwilling to trust themselves much ashore, dreading that the mischievous natives might choose to retaliate when they had them as strangers in their power.

While lying in the harbour of Toloo, where the ship was painted and prepared for a lengthened voyage, the missionaries determined on first sailing for the Friendly Islands, and then to return by the Marquesas, where the remaining two of the missionaries designed to settle. Returning for the present again to Tahiti on the twenty-sixth, to see how their friends were, they found them in excellent health and spirits, and every thing wearing a promising aspect. Setting sail again on the same afternoon, and accompanied out of the bay of Matavai by many canoes filled with the friendly natives, they were soon off the land again, and fairly at sea on their voyage to Tongatabu.

Sailing on to the south of the Society Islands, they passed in sight of several of them. Visiting that circular cluster of islets discovered by Captain Cook on his second voyage, called Palmerston's Island, they had a sight of the beautiful submarine grotto which that adventurous navigator has so well described. It consists of fanciful shoots of many sorts of coral, seen perfectly at the bottom of the glassy sea, and glowing with colours that no art can imitate, realizing all that the imagination has ever conceived of the haunts of mermaids, and the gods of the deep.

The islands themselves are united by reefs of coral rock, and clad in their inner recesses with nut and other trees. The missionaries landed on one of the islets, but their time did not allow them to prosecute further discoveries. Sailing on, therefore, and passing several other islands, on Sunday the ninth of April, they saw and stood in for the harbour of Tongatabu.

In sailing into the extensive harbour of this island, our voyagers were followed by several boats filled with natives, but one in particular struck their attention from its size, and its having on board about six persons. This vessel carried a large sail, which the natives managed so well, that it shot far a-head of the Duff with all her canvass set. The navigators, then slackening sail, and falling astern, seemed to wait triumphantly for the approach of the ship. When the Duff had cast anchor, the applications to get on board were so numerous, that sentinels were required on deck to keep off all but a very few; amongst whom a great chief, named Futtafaihe, a man of stately gait and noble manner, who appeared about forty years of age, was introduced to Captain Wilson. The missionaries were much disconcerted on finding that these islanders spoke a language quite different from those at Tahiti; and though their chief talked a good deal, all that could be collected from his speech was, that he was a very great man, and that there were some white men upon the island whom he promised to bring to the ship on the following day.

These white men proved to be two English sailors, who had left their ship about thirteen months before, and who had been nearly all this time in Tongatabu. The account that they gave of the disposition of the natives, was not very encouraging, so far as the safety either of the lives or properties of the missionaries was concerned. Iron tools, in particular, presented as was reported, a temptation to these mischievous and subtle islanders, which they could hardly be long expected to resist. Indeed, their conduct on board the Duff, and various attempts they made upon her, with the view, it appeared, of driving her upon the rocks in some dark and stormy night were very alarming; and it required all the vigilance of Captain Wilson and his men to protect themselves and their ship.

The common natives seemed to stand greatly in awe of the chiefs, who were much better disposed towards the strangers than their thievish subjects. The only chance, therefore, for the ten missionaries, who still persisted in their determination to settle on the island, was to place themselves under the protection of the chiefs, as the two European fugitives advised them.

One of these, named Toogahowe, the most powerful chieftain in the island, and the terror of all the other chiefs of Tongatabu, seemed the most proper personage to become the protector of the Mission. This powerful islander was about forty years of age, possessing great personal strength, and of a sullen and morose countenance. To this man the missionaries determined to trust themselves; as he expressed a readiness to receive them kindly, and to give them a house to live in, and land for their use.

When this chief came on board the Duff, the awe-struck natives almost fled at his approach; an effect which was gratifying to the anxious men, who now looked to him as their protector. Captain Wilson, however, in the presence of the missionaries, and with Ambler, one of the Englishmen found on the island, for his interpreter, thought it necessary to explain personally to this chief all the particulars of the intention of the missionaries in seeking to settle on his island; observing, that these men had come across the sea thus far, solely for the good of the native people, and to instruct them in various important matters of religion. Though great pains were taken to make these disinterested views of the Europeans, plain to the savage chieftain, it was evident that he did not fully comprehend them. He expressed, however, in reply, sufficient to show that he understood great part of what was said. Again offering the missionaries a house, and liberty to do as they pleased, if they chose to put themselves under his protection, he said he would, on the same afternooon, send a double canoe to take their baggage on shore.

This promise was punctually performed. The canoe, on its arrival at the ship, was instantly loaded, and seven of the missionaries, accompanied by Ambler the interpreter, and a petty chief, embarked with the baggage, and proceeding westward in the bay, to a place called Aheefo, at length effected a landing at a considerable distance from the ship. Their progress to the home provided for them, was, however, more toilsome and tedious than they had imagined.

The canoe was deeply laden, and a flat projected into the sea where they had to land, so that they could not get the boat within half a mile of the dry beach. All this distance they were obliged to wade up to the knees, carrying their goods ; and, in addition to this trouble, they found that the house appointed for them was situated above a mile beyond the beach. Six hours were the missionaries and the natives employed in this fatiguing business. The assistance of the latter was of much service, and not an article of the property was stolen, although night overtook them in the midst of their toil. It was an hour past midnight before every thing was safely got in, and they were left to themselves in their new habitation. The weary missionaries then commended themselves to God, whose presence had followed them even to the islands of the South Sea, and lay down to rest for the first time, in that spot among the heathen in which they had chosen to dwell.

Never, however, had the missionaries slept sounder in their lives, than they did that night in their new house in Tongatabu. On their awaking, the natives had a breakfast prepared for them, according to the fashion of the country. Having partaken of this, they returned to the ship; and in the course of the day landed the whole of their property: after they had begun to settle themselves in the island, the Duff prepared for her departure for the Marquesas. Before setting sail, the ship was visited by a woman of rank from the island, a remarkably corpulent lady, who was attended by many chiefs and a great retinue of females. The respect paid to this stout gentlewoman, even by the men, and the treatment that females in general received here, differing as it did from their degraded condition in islands seemingly in other respects farther advanced in civilization, was a matter which struck the missionaries much, and induced them to form good expectations of their new neighbours.

On the fourteenth, the morning being delightful, the Duff again got under weigh, and on the following day was clear of the island and its reefs; when the navigators, rejoicing in a fair wind, and good sea room, proceeded cheerily on the remainder of their voyage.

CHAPTER IV.

The Duff arrives at Santa Christina. Visit of seven beautiful females. State of the island. Landing of two missionaries. Curiosity and kindness of the natives. Their feelings. Anecdote of a native who stole from the ship. Adventures of Mr. Harris. Firmness of Mr. Crook. The Duff sails for Tahiti.

A little before sunrise, on the eleventh of June, the Captain of the Duff descried Santa Christina, one of the Marquesan islands. In the course of the voyage, he had passed several islands, on one of which several of the crew landed. This party was unable to get back on account of the dangerous surf on the beach, and was obliged to remain all night on the shore without shelter. They encountered no small peril from the reefs of coral before they finally reached the ship. The whole passage was rough and stormy, but they thought all their toil amply repaid when they arrived at the place of their destination, and anchored safely in Resolution bay.

Their first visitors from the shore were seven beautiful females, who swam towards the ship, with no garments but a plaiting of green leaves about their waist, and remained gamboling in the water for nearly three hours. Upon the invitation of some of the native men, who were by this time in the ship, they were prevailed upon to go on board. The chief of the island came on board soon after the females.

He had a thoughtful countenance, and had two brothers who strikingly resembled him ; all seemed oppressed with care. Yet did they, as well as the women, sometimes burst into fits of extravagant laughter, a practice not uncommon with those who are by habit melancholy. At those times they would talk as fast as their tongues could rattle. This chief seemed to have strange ideas of the European musket, and seeing one lying on the deck of the Duff, he carried it carefully to the Captain, and begged him anxiously 'to put it to sleep.'

Provisions seemed to be much less plentiful on this island, than on the luxurious shores of Tahiti, and the natives frequently complained of hunger while on board the Duff. To some a little meat was occasionally given, which the men would uniformly take away from the females and apply to their own use. The women, and others who had no canoes, remained on board the ship nearly the whole of the day; and when evening drew nigh, they leaped one by one over the side into the sea, and swam like fishes, in a body to the shore.

The two missionaries, who had destined themselves for this island, were a Mr. Crook and a Mr. Harris. When the chief, whose name was Tenae, was informed by the Captain of the intention of two Englishmen to settle among his people for their instruction, the good natured barbarian was highly delighted; and offering them a house to live in, he also promised a share of all that he possessed.

The two missionaries afterwards going on shore to reconnoitre the place, Tenae received them on the beach, and conducted them a little way with much decorum. He was evidently proud of the visit, and desiring to show off the strangers to the natives who crowded round, he made them all halt and form a ring round the objects of their curiosity; those in front sitting down to allow the others to see over their heads. The sister of the chief, allowing her natural curiosity to get the better of her sense of decorum, or of her obedience to her brother, did not readily comply with the order delivered, and a reproof from him, which was the consequence, affected the poor girl to tears.

When the chief had exhibited the missionaries in this manner to the people, for about a quarter of an hour, he conducted them up the valley, to show them the house which he intended for their reception. When they reached it they found it small and mean, compared with the lofty building that their brethren occupied in Tahiti; and all the food that was set before them was a few cocoa nuts. The chief, however, and the people in general seemed disposed to treat them with every kindness. Mr. Harris was discouraged by the poorness of the accommodations, and his ardor in the cause was insufficient to induce him to submit to them.

On the afternoon of the following day, Mr.

Crook landed again, taking with him his bed and some clothes. As Harris declined for the present to go on shore, some of the ship's people went with Crook; and a boy, whom the Captain brought from Tahiti, was left to keep him company for the night. Tenae, the chief, again receiving the strangers at the beach, conducted them up the valley towards the house as before, and treated them throughout with perfect kindness and respect.

They found the valley to abound with fruit trees of various sorts, besides the cocoa nut, the ahee nut, and the bread fruit. Orchards, filled with these and other trees, were even inclosed within walls of stones, built loosely upon each other and formed into squares; these fence walls being often six feet in height. It was late before the officer, who conducted this expedition, was enabled to return to the ship; and refusing, on account of the lateness of the hour, to take the chief's brother on board, the sensitive islander was so hurt in his feelings, as to give way to tears.

Mr. Crook, the missionary, continued to remain contentedly on shore, assimilating himself as much as possible to the habits of the natives, and eating the sour mahie, and other coarse viands offered him, without a murmur. This conduct so won the heart of the generous chief, that he adopted him as his own son; an act held by these islanders in the most sacred respect.

While the Duff lay in the harbour, the common natives had given various indications of that thievish disposition so general among the islanders of the South Sea. On the thirteenth of the month, while the ship's company were at dinner, one of the natives stole an iron article called a pump-bolt, but before he could get off with this trifling prize, he was detected by the gunner and another, and prevented from making his escape.

On seeing this, others of his countrymen, who at this time crowded the ship's deck, all jumped overboard and swam to the shore. The unfortunate thief was seized and lashed to the shrouds; and a loaded musket being brought out before him, he fully expected to be presently shot.

Soon after, a young man arrived from the

shore in a canoe, having brought with him a present of two pigs, with a leaf of the plantain, which he presented to the Captain, and earnestly entreated pardon for the offender, who was his own father. But the Captain refused to yield the petition of the distressed islander, and would not accept his proffered present.

The scene that now took place between the father and son was most affecting. They kissed and embraced each other, and took what they considered a last farewell, with deep feeling and evident anguish of mind. This was more than the benevolent Captain was able to endure. Taking up the loaded musket he discharged it into the air, and then gave orders for the release of the prisoner.

The bewildered man could now hardly believe that he was not shot, and that he was to be set at liberty. When he found himself free, and was presented to his son, both were dumb with the consternation of joy. But the Captain would take none of the son's presents, and only warning the offender to beware of similar acts in future, he sent them both away with the pigs and the plantain leaf; and they set off rejoicing in his clemency and magnanimity.

Mr. Harris made one more attempt to gather courage for a settlement on the island. But he became alarmed and after passing one night there, on the following evening at dusk he dragged his chest and other articles down to the shore, in the hope of finding a boat to carry him back to the ship. At that time, however, no boat was near the beach, and the ship was too far out to answer his hail. Determined not to go back to the chief's house, he sat down on the chest, with the purpose of remaining all night where he was.

Here he continued, with much discomfort, until about four in the morning, when several o the natives crowded round him; and showing, to his apprehension, strong symptoms, not only o a wish to help themselves to his baggage, but to assault his person, the poor man became more terrified than ever.

In order to steal his clothes while in this situation, the natives, according to his own account, drove him from the chest; upon which he fled to the hills in the utmost consternation. Here he was afterwards found in a most pitiable condition, and almost out of his senses with fear; having been sought out by one of the ship's company, who, upon the news of the disaster reaching the ship, was sent on shore to endeavour to trace him.

Bringing him back to the beach where his chest was still safe, the sailors found the surf by this time so high, that they could not get the ship's boat ashore. So in order to deliver the poor missionary from the apprehended dangers of the island, tying a rope round his body, and also round the chest, they hauled both through the surf to the boat, and at last had them carried safe to the ship.

The experience which Mr. Crook had acquired on the island, led him to conclusions directly contrary to those of the cowardly Harris. Finding that Captain Wilson was preparing to depart, he intimated his resolution to stay on the island, with no other companions save the kind hearted chieftain and his friends.

This worthy young man, having had the good

sense to accommodate himself, as far as possible, to the feelings and circumstances of the islanders, undertook their instruction with perfect cheerfulness. Though sensible that the conversation and sympathy of a christian missionary from his own country, would be a great comfort to him in these regions of igorance, yet as that was denied, he was willing, in the strength of his divine Master, to labour alone, while there was any prospect of doing good among the people.

Taking with him, therefore, an assortment of garden seeds to sow in the valley, with some implements of husbandry, some medicines, books, and other useful articles, he contentedly prepared for his solitary labours.

Before the departure of the Duff, the Captain, for the first time went on shore in the island. On landing, he was surrounded by a crowd of the natives, who were delighted with the honour of his company in their village. Having partaken of some refreshment in the house of the chief, the party proceeded inland towards the mountains, the upper ridge of which they were very desirous of reaching.

The asçent was, in some places so difficult, that only one of the Englishmen and the chief, were able to reach it. The view from the top of the mountain, however, well rewarded the travellers for their trouble. Besides the [illegible]tic valleys of their own island spread out beneath them, the two adventurers saw all the other five Marquesan islands, rising up out of the bosom of the surrounding ocean.

Tenae, the chief, as they stood on the narrow summit of the mountain, requested the Englishman to fire his musket in the direction of Trevenan's island, now lying beneath them. When the other had done this, the chief seemed to be greatly delighted, as he listened to the echoes of the shot repeated and resounding among the mountains.

On the same evening, when the party had reached the beach, the Captain and his friends took a farewell of the chief, and of Mr. Crook, the intrepid and youthful missionary. The conduct of the latter was, on this occasion, as manly and gallant as it had all along been.

Betraying no sign of fear at being left alone by

FAREWELL TO MR. CROOK.

Page 55.

his friends, nor any way daunted by the work he had undertaken, 'the tears glistened in his eyes,' says one of the journals, 'but none fell;' and he resigned himself to the care of Him, by whom he knew he should not be forsaken.

On the morning of the twenty-seventh of June, the day following that on which the Captain had taken leave of Mr. Crook, he weighed anchor, and set sail. He directed his course to Tahiti, as he felt some anxiety to ascertain in what circumstances he might find those, whom he had left there three months before.

Having cleared the harbour of Santa Christina, those on board saw, on the twenty-eighth, several lights upon a neighbouring island, and some canoes with natives shortly after reached the ship. On the third of July they obtained a sight of the nearest to them of the Society islands; and on the sixth, about noon, the Duff was again between the romantic highlands of Matavai bay, in the island of Tahiti.

CHAPTER V.

Occurrences at Tahiti. The sawpit and blacksmith's shop. A romantic valley. Building of a boat. Difficulties of acquiring the language. Thievishness of the natives. Robbery of the blacksmith's shop. Prosperity of the Mission, and arrival of the Duff.

THE first step of the missionaries in Tahiti after the departure of the Duff, on the voyage which we have just described, and after suitably preparing their own house, was to erect a sawpit for cutting timber, and a blacksmith's forge, for the fitting and manufacture of their iron implements.

In these necessary labours the natives gave them every assistance, and when they saw them cut a tree into a great number of thin deals, they were greatly astonished: never before having an idea that a tree could be subdivided lengthwise into more than two parts.

Finding that they wanted thick planks for the blacksmith's shop, the missionaries informed the king. Upon which, saying only, '*Harry-mie,*' in his language, meaning in English, 'come along,' one of them went with him to see where he had the wood, he taking with him six of his men, besides the one on whose shoulders he sat.

The king started forth up the valley behind the settlement, and entering every house on his way, he searched for and took what wood he wanted, whether the owners were at home or not. Some of the people resisted, but the king and his men took all the planks they could find; and when remonstrated with by the missionaries, he only replied, that it was the custom of the country.

All this time, the king dared not to alight, in justice to his subjects; for, according to another custom, every place on whieh he sets his foot is made sacred, and becomes his own. The man that carried him, however, taking him through places where he ran the risk every moment of breaking his neck, arrived at length upon his own property.

His majesty now alighted upon the ground, and, taking a stride or two, asked the missionary, with much complacency, if that was the manner in which King George of England walked? Being answered in the affirmative, he was highly pleased, and continued to stalk on for several miles, although the rain poured down the whole time.

When he had tired himself with this exercise, making the missionary a present of a hog, he suffered him to depart; being now in high good humour with himself, for so much resembling King George of England.

Those natives, who lived in the near neighbourhood of the missionaries, having now learned to speak many English words, the latter set about teaching them the alphabet, as they appeared quite eager to learn to read. Others of the missionaries were employed in building additional houses.

While all these various works were going on, five of them, to please their adventurous friend, Haamanemane, the old priest, agreed to accompany him to the neighbouring island of Eimeo, there to finish the schooner which he had long been building. Setting off, therefore, they found this island quite as romantic as Captain Cook had described it, the mountains round the edge of it having the appearance of the ruins of a stupendous fortification.

About this time, some of those remaining in Tahiti, going inland for wood, had occasion to explore a most romantic valley. They found it to run up between lofty and almost perpendicular mountains, to the length of about seven miles, whilst the breadth, at the foot of the mountains averaged only a quarter of a mile.

Through this long and verdant pass, a river slowly and silently meanders. At the bottom of the valley there is a little descent, and a light breeze sweeps down it continually. The sides of the mountains are almost covered with trees and shrubs, among which, a grey coloured bird, resembling a thrush, makes the groves musical with its everlasting song. Parrots and parroquets innumerable, with the most beautiful plumage, enliven the beauty and romance of the scene.

In this happy valley, there are numbers of the natives who only see the sun a few hours in the day; his beams being intercepted by the lofty mountains, leaving a misty shadow, almost resembling a soft twilight, as the prevailing light of this pleasing spot. These indolent people, living among plantations bearing every vegetable luxury the rich earth affords in these regions, scarcely take the trouble of gathering the fruit, that drops plentifully around them.

When the blacksmith's forge was quite completed, and the man employed began his work, nothing could exceed the delight and astonishment with which the natives beheld his operations. To see shapeless bars, and pieces of iron, speedily turned into the most useful tools by the blowing of the fire, and the beating of the hammer, was to them like a miracle. Even some of the chiefs, when they saw the sparks fly from the metal, while it was struck upon the anvil, instantly fled, from the notion that it was spitting at them; and others were particularly alarmed by hearing it hiss in the water. But Pomare, the chief, and father of the king, was not a man to be so easily frightened.

Going into the smithy one day, when the blacksmith was at work, he stood for a time

THE FORGE.

Page 65.

gazing in wonder at the transformations of art, until, quite transported at what he saw, he eagerly embraced the sweating workman, touching noses with him according to the custom of the country.

The missionaries readily procured servants among the natives. Having cut a sufficient quantity of wood into thin planks, and other forms, they constructed a flat-bottomed boat, for the purpose of crossing with goods the shallows at the mouth of the river, that passed beside the spot on which the principal house of the new settlers was situated.

Of this boat the working part of the missionaries were justly proud. She measured twenty-two feet in length on the rim, six in breadth in her centre, and her general breadth was two feet six inches. This vessel, considered to be about six tons burden, was launched with great ceremony on the last day of May, with forty of the natives, besides some of the missionaries on board.

But to the simple Tahitians the new-fashioned canoe was nothing, compared to the cuckoo clock, which the strangers had brought with them, and erected in their house, and which at first struck even the chiefs with astonishment and terror. An old chief actually brought the wooden bird some food, from an apprehension that the missionaries were disposed to starve it. The king himself was so struck with admiration at its mechanism, that he expressed bitter regret at the comparative ignorance of his own people, and those who could fashion such an astonishing machine.

Among the labours of the missionaries at this early period, that in which they found the greatest difficulty, was the correct attainment of the language of the natives. In this they had but little assistance from the ignorant Swedes, whom at first they had used as interpreters; and the printed specimens of the Tahitian language, which they had obtained in England, having been hastily set down by casual visitors, were so incorrect that they proved to be little better than perplexing puzzles. Still they persevered, writing down their respective observations, until their endeavours were crowned with success, and the language of Tahiti was transferred to books for the use of the inhabitants. This was the first of the Polynesian dialects, which the industry of missionary labourers had reduced to writing.

During the progress of these labours, the colonists met with many annoyances. One of their own number treated the natives badly, and prevailed upon the Swedes to refuse to interpret. A pilfering disposition of the natives was another source of great trouble; as these islanders seemed to place more value upon a useless thing which they had stolen, than a useful article given them in barter.

Even the king himself seemed now to encourage, for his own gratification, a little ingenious thieving from his new subjects, who had come to his island possessed of so many desirable things. With this intent, he craftily recommended a new set of servants to the Missionaries, desiring them at the same time to discharge their present ones, who, he assured them, were arrant thieves. But the missionaries suspected that his majesty's servants would be still greater thieves, and rejected his proposal without ceremony. About this time, one of them was so audacious as to steal the clothes of Mr. Gilham, the surgeon of the mission, as he went in to bathe.

The thief fled, and on being pursued, was traced to a house, where the pursuers heard the sound of the native drum, and learned that a large company were assembled. The missionaries, nothing daunted, rushed at once into the house, and found the culprit in the midst of the assembly, finely dressed in the surgeon's clothes, and prepared to entertain his companions with a dance. The whole of those assembled, to the number of a hundred, rose in confusion.

Conscious of countenancing the exploit of their companion, they all fled, while the delinquent was seized in his fine dress, and being stripped, was brought in triumph to Point Venus, and chained to a pillar of the house. The fellow, however, soon contrived to free himself, and ran off, carrying the padlock with which he had been confined, but being taken a second time, the padlock was recovered, and he was sent about his business.

About this time, a box was stolen, merely for the sake of the nails that held it together. This, however, was nothing to the robbery of the blacksmith's shop. The native who committed this depredation, might have effected an entrance, with great ease, into that place, by merely cutting the slight wattles of the boards by which it was built.

Preferring, however, the more difficult way, he dug into the earth several feet on the outside of the building; then burrowing for himself a hole through the ground which went under the wall, he rose through the floor of the house, and taking with him several iron articles of value, escaped.

Some differences of opinion had occurred among the missionaries, during the time of the Duff's absence, but not such as materially to affect their ordinary proceedings. They kept up their religious exercises, and often addressed the natives through the interpreter, in the presence of the King and Queen, and old Haamanemane. Rules were drawn up for the labours which were to occupy each day of the week.

A bell was rung at six in the morning. Half an hour afterwards, the colonists assembled for morning prayer, laboured till ten, when they breakfasted, and then spent the time till dinner in various studies. At seven in the evening their bell again rang, for evening prayers, after which the journal of the day was read aloud, and all retired to rest.

The mission had thus far prospered exceedingly. All employed in it enjoyed good health. The seeds which they planted on the island had begun to spring up; one of the sheep brought over with them had produced its first lamb; their English pigs had already began to multiply; and a nest of six rabbits was also added to their stock, and promised soon to overrun the neighbouring valleys. Shortly before the return of the Duff, the colony was increased by the birth of a female child; a circumstance which gave much pleasure to the missionaries, and excited the astonishment of the natives.

While these things were going on, one morning, a great shout from the natives drew the attention of the colonists towards the bay, where the white sails of the returning Duff appeared already in sight. They immediately went off to meet her in their flat-bottomed boat, and many were the congratulations and inquiries that passed between the parties. The return of the Duff to Tahiti, for the last time before her final departure for Europe, brings us now to the point with which we concluded the foregoing chapter.

CHAPTER VI.

The Duff leaves Tahiti. Touches at Huahine. Anecdote of the Irishman. Arrival at Tongatabu. Captain Cook's well. Wonderful coral rock. Large house. Death of the king. Funeral ceremonies. Progress of the colonists. Earthquake. Character and manners of the natives. Departure of the Duff. She strikes upon a coral reef. Her arrival in England.

After dividing a portion of their cargo among the settlers at Tahiti, and assisting them to build a good sized vessel to cruise about the neighbouring islands, the officers of the Duff were again ready for sea. Intending to touch again at Tongatabu, with the remainder of the cargo, intended for the missionaries, Captain Wilson took an affecting farewell of the colonists, and on the fourth of August finally set sail for Europe.

On the day after leaving Tahiti, the Duff found herself off the neighbouring island of Huahine; at that time harassed continually by the wars of the restless natives. When the Duff drew near, a number of the inhabitants came on board. Among them was an Irishman by the name of Connor, who had been shipwrecked there, and of whom the missionaries had before heard, at Tongatabu.

When Captain Wilson came to speak to this man, he found, to his astonishment, that he had so forgotten his native tongue, that if he began a sentence in English, he hesitated, and was obliged to finish it in the language of the islands. He, as well as the natives who accompanied him, strongly urged the English captain to go ashore and make some stay at their island. This not being agreed to, the Irishman requested to be taken home to England. For though he had a wife and a child on the island, he considered his life and theirs in continual jeopardy, from the cruel wars of the natives.

Going on shore, however, to take a final leave of his wife and child, the poor Irishman found that, like many others of his countrymen, he had a warmer heart than even he himself suspected. Overcome to tears by the sight of his infant, a beautiful baby nine months old, after going and returning to the ship, carrying the child all the time in his arms, his affection at last entirely prevailed. Informing the Captain that he found it impossible to leave his infant, and that its mother could not consent to part with it, he returned to pass his days with this savage people, rather than be separated from his wife and his offspring.

Having set sail from Huahine, the Duff, on the eighteenth of the same month, again cast anchor in the large harbour of Tongatabu. One of the missionaries who came off to the ship, gave information of their general health, and of their having found it necessary to separate themselves during the absence of the ship, and to live in parties of two or three, under the protection of different chiefs.

This necessary precaution, however, having deprived them of the advantages of association, they were not making that progress in the purposes of the mission, nor even in learning the language, which their brethren at Tahiti had done. In other respects, the occurrences which had taken place at the two islands were very similar.

Most of the chiefs treated their new friends with kindness. One of them, named Fattafaihe, received the missionaries very hospitably. Taking them to the beach, near which his house was situated, and pointing to a group of small islands which lay in sight, he advised them to select one for their residence, and their property. At the same time, he added, that any thing they might choose was entirely at their service.

Landing next day on one of these islands, the missionaries were shown a well, which had been dug by Captain Cook. It was both large and deep, but its water was by no means good. Having crossed to another island, in which they found large numbers of cocoa-nut, plantain, and bread-fruit trees as well as sugar canes, and good fresh water, they came upon a curiosity which is worthy to be noticed. This was a peculiarly shaped coral rock, standing upon the beach, which rose to the height of five feet, was four feet thick, and formed like the stump of an old tree.

This remarkable piece of coral was much perforated with holes, in which were numbers of water snakes, about thirty inches long, with skins beautifully variegated. These the natives would not allow to be touched, calling them agees, or sacred animals.

Their bodies were ornamented by nature with alternate circles of black and white, from the tail to the head; each ring being about half an inch in breadth, relieved along the back by a beautiful streak of blue. Though not poisonous, these snakes were represented to be very dangerous, the natives saying that they would kill a man by twisting themselves round his neck, and then biting a hole in his throat.

During their travels through this island, the missionaries found here also a house, that was

6

one hundred and eighteen feet long, and fifty-six wide, and thatched with great neatness. Several beautiful spots, and large groves of cocoa-nut trees, extending as far as the cliffs above the sea, were also observed upon the island, with pleasant springs of fresh water. One of these gushed out from the recesses of a rocky cavern, into which the sea flowed at high water.

The face of the country in this island is generally level. Before some of the houses of the natives, are handsome green areas, and they cultivate and fence their lands in a very neat manner. Near the houses they generally lay out their lands in fields or small inclosures, the whole being named an abbey, and surrounded by trenches into which these fences are set.

The fences are made of reeds plaited close together, and supported by stakes of the banana or some other tree, at short distances, which, taking root, form a sort of hedge rows, bearing fruit. In these fields, the natives cultivate their great favourite, the Ava root, yams, and other vegetables.

Shortly after the arrival of the missionaries in

Tongatabu, an event occurred which made them early acquainted with many of the most remarkable customs of the natives. This event was the illness and death of the old king of the island, who was a good man, and had long been held in great esteem by his subjects. While he was at the point of death, the chief, who acted as admiral of the fleet, set sail in a large double canoe, on a voyage which could not take up less time than two months, to bring what he called a spirit, to cure the illness of the king.

The ceremonies observed by the natives at the funeral of the king, who soon after died as was expected, were truly savage, and, in some respects, horrible. Two of the wives of the deceased were now devoted to be strangled at the tomb. Walking together in the mournful, or rather frightful procession, which followed the body; one of these devoted women wept bitterly at the idea of her fate, while the other evinced but little concern. The relatives of the late king cutting themselves with the shark's tooth, as they went, until the blood streamed down their faces, presented to the missionaries a hideous appearance.

At the actual interment of the body, which did not take place for several days after this, the scene that presented itself round the grave was still more dreadful. Meantime the numbers that crowded from all quarters, into the valley where the body was to be buried, were prodigious, and filled the missionaries with considerable alarm; as they were informed that this vast body might make a stay in the place for two or three months, if the enormous quantity of provisions that was also pouring in, should last so long, and that during this time all sorts of excesses were likely to occur.

The burying place of the king was situated in a rich valley, and consisted of a cleared area of about four acres. In the centre of this, rose a mound with a gentle slope, and on the top of the mound, under an open shed, was the tomb, entirely built of coral stone. On the day of the funeral, above four thousand persons sat around this area. A great shouting and blowing of conch or trumpet shells, was the first part of the ceremony.

After this, about a hundred men rushed hastily

into the area from without, and being armed with clubs and spears, began to cut and mangle themselves in a shocking manner, numbers of them striking their own heads with their clubs, until the blood streamed down, the blows being heard among all the confusion at a distance of thirty or forty yards. Some, who had spears, thrust them through their thighs, arms, and cheeks, all the time calling on the deceased by name in the most affecting tones of grief.

One man, who had been a servant of the deceased, appeared on this occasion to be quite frantic. Having first oiled his hair, he entered the area carrying fire in his hand, which he soon applied to his head, and ran about with the hair all in flames. Some knocked out their teeth with stones; the shell blowers cut their heads with their shells; and the missionaries saw with horror a man running round the area, with a spear sticking through the flesh of his arm.

Unable any longer to bear this frightful scene, the missionaries left it, and on returning about two hours after, they found the area still filled with people, who continued successively to cut and mangle themselves. Shortly after, on again coming close to this barbarous exhibition, they heard at a distance a murmur of female voices, giving out low and mournful sounds, expressive of the deepest sorrow and lamentation.

Presently, the now empty area began to be filled by a procession of nearly a hundred and fifty women, who moved slowly, and in Indian file, each carrying a basket of coral sand. Then followed about eighty men in the same manner, who sang, as they marched carrying their sand, a strain, the words of which imported, 'This is a blessing to the dead,' to which were added the voices of a third company of women bearing a quantity of cloth. This was the most interesting part of the ceremony.

The three bands thus walked towards the tomb, the canopy over which was covered entirely with black cloth, as was also the body, now brought forward on a bier. When the corpse of the king was deposited in the tomb, seven men blew a blast upon their conch-shells, and then a strain was raised by the singers, deeply expressive of heartfelt grief.

Another party of men now entered the area, who went on cutting and wounding themselves as before, and were followed by sixteen mourners of the king's family, each of whom had cut his little fingers off. Successive scenes of singing and sorrow followed this, after which the multitude sat awhile in deep silence ; then rising up, and giving a great shout, and tearing off the wreaths of leaves with which they had been decorated for mourning, they quietly dispersed to hold their feasting in other parts.

These great gatherings, which brought to this spot many even of the inhabitants of the neighbouring islands, were considered, by the new settlers, as upon the whole, exceedingly favourable to the purposes of the mission. An opportunity was thus afforded of addressing strangers from distant quarters, and testifying against these cruel enormities ; a proceeding which was not altogether without its effect.

Pressing invitations to settle in several of the neighbouring islands were given to the missionaries, which nothing but ignorance of their language prevented them from accepting. Among their other labours, one of their number, a Mr. Bowell, whom they had made their secretary, was assiduously employed in forming a vocabulary of the language of Tongatabu, in which he was much assisted by the ingenuity and zeal of the native chiefs themselves.

With respect to the progress of the colonists, in their agricultural labours, their peas and beans rose well, and in two months were in fine bloom; but the crop of these, and some other vegetables, never came to maturity, being totally destroyed by the rats and mice with which the island appeared to swarm.

The waste of provisions by the natives during the feastings, which followed the death of the king, caused a natural apprehension among the missionaries of a season of great scarcity. The abundance of fish, however, which were easily obtained on the shores of the island, was a perpetual safeguard from the calamity of famine.

Early one morning, while it was yet dark, the missionaries were greatly alarmed by a shock of an earthquake, during which the earth trembled beneath them so long and so sensibly, that it put them all in the greatest consternation. The poor natives near them were also quite panic-struck, increasing the general terror by setting up loud cries, while the surf on the beach rose with fury, and made a noise that seemed dreadful. The natives imputed this effect to the Atua, or spirit, who frequently alarms them by such visitations, but when the shock is over they quickly forget it, though it is sometimes so violent as to prostrate the trees and houses on the island.

Notwithstanding the savage practices to which we have alluded, the missionaries found these islanders to possess, upon the whole, all the excellent and even amiable qualities, for which the various navigators by whom they had been visited had given them credit. If they are in general dishonest to strangers, their honesty among themselves is unimpeachable.

Like the inhabitants of Tahiti, they exercise a hospitality and a generosity to the strangers from whom, at the same time, they might occasionally pilfer. Among themselves, were they dying of hunger, the first morsel any of them

SPORTS OF THE ISLANDERS.

Page 85.

might receive, would be instantly and cheerfully divided with the one nearest him, who might not have been so fortunate as himself.

The soil of the island the missionaries found to be very rich and prolific, so that if the inhabitants were trained to industry, it might be made to yield great abundance. The people, though disposed to be more industrious than those of many other islands in the South Sea, yet spent most of their time sporting upon the waters, and diving under the surf; or in telling stories of their own invention, as they lay under the shade of their picturesque trees.

The curiosity which they shewed, however, in watching all the proceedings of the missionaries, gave hopes that the arts of civilization might soon be taught them; and the strong desire they expressed for articles of English manufacture, such as ironmongery, woollen cloths, and especially blankets, makes it probable that if any pains were taken to teach them, they would not be long in learning to manufacture for themselves.

The mission in this part of the world being

SPORTS OF THE ISLANDERS.

Page 85.

now pretty well established, the Captain of the Duff prepared to take a final leave of the island of Tongatabu, and to make sail for Europe, where he knew the friends of the undertaking were most anxiously waiting for his return.

On the seventh of September, therefore, having taken an affectionate farewell of all the missionaries, and commended them to that Providence, who was able to take care of them even among the islands of the South Sea, Captain Wilson weighed anchor, and was soon out in the ocean again, intending to sail first to China on his way back to England.

Captain Wilson and his men had not been long at sea, however, when, falling in with another group of islands, unknown to them, their ship became entangled among reefs and breakers, and at night struck upon a reef of coral, over which the sea was scarcely seen to break.

All hands rushed on deck, upon hearing the ship strike, and as she lay fast and beating upon the rock, the horrors of shipwreck, in these unknown seas, began to stare the poor mariners in the face. The darkness now seemed to offer only the alternative of being drowned, should they not be able to save the ship, or of falling in perhaps, with cannibal savages, whom their imaginations painted in all their fierceness and cruelty.

This, however, was no time for indulging fear, but for energetic action. Setting the sails quickly aback, therefore, the sea being fortunately tolerably smooth, they were not long in getting her off; and when the seamen found their ship again afloat, they could scarcely believe in their sudden deliverance from such imminent danger.

Sailing from China about the beginning of the year 1798, she had a prosperous voyage homewards, touching at the Cape of Good Hope on the seventeenth of March; and on the twenty-third of June the voyagers again had a sight of the coast of Ireland. Putting into Cork harbour, they were obliged to wait there eight days for a convoy, and at last, on the eleventh of July, they cast anchor in the river Thames.

Thus ended the first and most remarkable missionary voyage that has yet been made out of England. The sensation created, by the favourable accounts of the mission, and the general promising aspect of the cause of religion in the islands of the South Sea, was very great, among all who had taken an interest in the adventure.

It was a topic of universal discussion, and excited a general and warm hope of success; the day seemed to have arrived when the heathen darkness which had brooded over those beautiful islands was to be dispelled by the bright sunshine of Christianity.

CHAPTER VII.

Second voyage of the Duff. Her fate. Adventures of Mr. Jefferson and other missionaries at Tahiti. Arrival of the Nautilus. Subsequent disasters. Ill treatment, and extreme perils of Mr. Jefferson and his companions. Deserters protected by the king.

THE accounts brought to England by the Duff, of the great success of her first voyage to the South Sea, and the exceedingly promising state of the mission, so elated its friends and supporters at home, that no time was lost in preparing to send out the ship a second time, with a large reinforcement of missionary strength.

The liberality, with which individuals came forward to patronize this work, was at least creditable to their feelings; and by the following December, and within a few months after her arrival at home, the Duff was again ready for sea. She had on board a cargo of every thing necessary, and twenty-nine additional missionaries; ten of whom were married and took with them their families.

The Duff was now commanded by a Captain Robson, and, sailing in the course of the same month, was soon far on her voyage towards Rio Janeiro. She had been out about two months, when, one fine morning as she drew near to the coast of Brazil, a sail was dimly perceived on the horizon.

Although it was then a time of war with France, this sight gave the missionaries no concern, as they little expected to find any hostile ship cruising in these latitudes. Paying no attention, therefore, the ship bore down towards them the same afternoon, but as there was little wind, it was evening before she came near to the Duff.

The moon was now up and shone brightly over the sea. Slight squalls began to arise, but still those on board were ignorant where the strange ship could be from, and why she had followed them all day. Great indeed was the consternation of the missionaries, when the vessel in chase began to fire upon them; and having been forced to heave too, they soon ascertained that this strange ship was a French privateer, and that the Duff with all on board was already her prize.

Their terror was now extreme, for a party of officers, boarding them from the French ship, and brandishing cutlasses over their heads, intimated that they must immediately go on board the Bonaparte,—for this was the privateer's name,—and remain there under hatches as prisoners. The anguish of the married men in being forced from their families, uncertain what was to be their future destiny, was indeed extreme.

They were not, however, allowed even a moment to indulge their feelings, but, together with the crew of the Duff, were driven, at the point of the cutlass, into the privateer's boats, like so many sheep, without an article of their property save what was on their backs.

What both parties of the captured suffered for several days afterwards, closed beneath the hatches, under the watch of strangers, and finding that all hopes of their voyage were at an end,—we cannot here dwell upon; nor can we follow them

PURSUIT OF THE DUFF.

Page 93.

in the troubles which they encountered during the remainder of this disastrous adventure.

Being carried into Monte Video, and there set on shore, they at length procured a vessel to convey them to Rio Janeiro, where they hoped to obtain a passage to England. But they had not been many days at sea before they were again captured by a Portugese man-of-war, and a second time separated into small parties and sent on board other and different ships. In such circumstances, the hardships they suffered were such as they were but ill prepared for, either by their principles, their habits, or their feelings; but their ultimate fate was to be carried back to Europe, and cast in a state of destitution on the streets of Lisbon. Having procured a passage back to England, the missionaries at length arrived in safety; with the loss, however, of every thing they possessed, and with completely frustrated purposes and anticipations. This happened just ten months from the time they had set sail with the brightest hopes, and noblest intentions.

This disastrous termination, to so favourite an

7

adventure, acted upon the Missionary Society at home like an electric shock; so little had its members anticipated any such result to their exertions. They had not recovered from the distress and disappointment which it occasioned, when the most alarming accounts arrived from the South Sea of the state of the original mission.

These accounts reported that eleven of the missionaries at first settled in Tahiti had been obliged, by the ill treatment of the natives, to leave the island and fly to Port Jackson; that three of those settled at Tongatábu had been cruelly murdered; that the rest had also found refuge at Port Jackson, whence they were probably now on their way to England; and that of those who had thus fled to New South Wales, one had been murdered near Port Jackson.

The consternation and grief that these tidings occasioned were so great, that the fire of missionary zeal seemed to have been almost extinguished in England. The natural despondency, occasioned by this train of misfortunes, was aggravated by the sneers of those who had originally condemned these adventures, as wild and extravagant. In order to explain briefly the cause of these latter events, we must now return to the several missionary settlements at first made in the South Sea.

To the covetous looks, which some of the natives of Tahiti often threw upon the little property of the missionaries in that island, we have already alluded. This feeling began to show itself in the young king, Otu, himself, shortly after the departure of the Duff from Tahiti; excited as he was by jealousy of the authority of Pomare, his father, and by the wicked suggestions of the two treacherous Swedes.

A patient continuance in well doing, on the part of Mr. Jefferson and his brethren, might in time have succeeded in banishing these jealousies, had not an event occurred that speedily brought on the most unforeseen consequences. In about a year after their first landing on the island, the missionaries were surprised one morning, by the arrival of a strange ship, being the first that had appeared since the departure of the Duff.

This was a vessel called the Nautilus, origi-ginally bound for the north-west coast of America, but which had been driven south by stormy weather, and was now reduced to great distress. Having nothing on board except muskets and powder, which they could barter for provisions with the natives of Tahiti, the latter, who by this time bad imbibed much of the mercenary spirit of Europeans, looked upon the intruders with that contempt, which the appearance of poverty so generally excites.

The missionaries, on the contrary, felt their distress, and assisted them with provisions, so that they were not obliged to sacrifice their scanty cargo to the cupidity of the king of Tahiti; who coveted their fire arms, with a view to the war-like purposes which then brooded in his mind. Having, with difficulty, got on board such supplies as the island afforded, chiefly by the aid of the missionaries, the Nautilus was soon again ready for sea.

On the fifth day after her arrival in the bay, she set sail from Tahiti, but the Captain was forced to leave behind him five natives of the

Sandwich Islands, whom he had taken and carried thus far, but who, having found means to escape from the ship, remained concealed somewhere on shore.

This unfortunate vessel, however, had not been gone from the island more than fourteen days, when, to the surprise of the missionaries, she again made her appearance in Matavai bay. Having encountered a severe gale off the neighbouring island of Huahine, she was obliged to put back for an increase of supplies; the Captain being forced also by these misfortunes, to alter his original destination, and to sail for Port Jackson, on the Australian Continent.

But, as if fated not only to suffer a series of troubles, but to be the means of bringing them upon others, the Nautilus, on the very night of her return to Tahiti, lost two of her crew, who escaped to the shore, and took with them the long boat, leaving the distressed Captain unable to proceed on his voyage, for want of sufficient men to work the ship.

In this dilemma, he again applied to his considerate friends, the missionaries, earnestly entreating them to use their interest with the king and chiefs of the island, to obtain their endeavours to secure and deliver up the deserters. Though this was an exceedingly delicate business, under the circumstances in which the missionaries were now placed, yet, considering the situation of the unfortunate Captain, they agreed to use their utmost interest to recover his men.

Besides their concern for the situation of the officers of the Nautilus, the missionaries were further induced to take a part in this matter, from a just alarm for themselves and their cause; foreseeing that, were any more profligate Englishmen left on the island, they might do much to defeat the purposes of the mission. Having succeeded, in recovering the ship's boat, which they sent to the Captain, they formed a party consisting of Mr. Jefferson and three others, to travel to the neighbouring district of Paré and there to wait upon the king and chiefs, respecting this business.

Proceeding on foot for several hours, the deputation at length reached the king's dwelling, and found his majesty surrounded by attendants, among whom they perceived the five Sandwich islanders who had formerly escaped from the ship. However imposing the king must have appeared, as he thus sat in regal state, his employment was not, to our notions, the most dignified; it being no other than that of cleansing a small tooth comb, with which he had probably been exercising himself in the usual way.

He received the missionary ambassadors with some politeness, touching noses, of course, in token of friendship, and he then asked them to what he was to attribute the honour of their visit. To this simple inquiry, the missionaries, thought fit to waive for the present any direct answer; and, in the mean time, sent for Pomare, the king's father, as well as Temaree, another chief, judging it best not to open their business before they were all three together.

After waiting for some time, during which the king's manner was by no means agreeable, the four missionaries resolved that they would themselves go and bring Pomare into his son's presence. Setting out, therefore, on this second journey, they had not proceeded quite a mile, when the affair all at once began to assume an alarming appearance.

The natives, in general, had saluted them as they passed, in their usual way; but a crowd of about thirty, gathering and following them, as they drew near to a river which it was necessary to cross, they were suddenly seized, each by three or four natives, who dragged them down hastily, and tore the clothes off their backs.

Two of them were left nearly naked, while the other two, who had also been partly stripped, were dragged by the hair of the head through the river, and almost drowned: the whole now expecting nothing else but to be instantly murdered.

The men who dragged Mr. Jefferson through the stream, seemed, with their companions, undetermined what to do with him. Some were for carrying him off to the mountains; others wanted to haul him down towards the sea; while a third party collected around, and endeavoured to rescue him from the hands of the assailants.

Meantime two of the others, who were stripped to the skin, were brought forward, and during the scuffle and dispute which followed, Mr. Jefferson prevailed upon the natives to carry them to the tent of Pomare, now not far distant. This at length they all consented to do, and as the missionaries passed along in this miserable predicament, the women came out and expressed their compassion with tears.

Arriving at the place where Pomare was, they were received by him and Idia his wife, with every attention ; and, being kindly supplied with cloth to cover themselves, were promised every protection that the chief could give. The three missionaries were still without their other companion, who had been parted from them during the scuffle, and for whom they now felt the utmost anxiety.

Pomare and his wife immediately offered to accompany them to Otu, the king. On their way thither they were again joined by their fourth companion, who had been dreadfully threatened by the natives, but was still safe, with the loss only of his hat and upper garments.

Pomare, on their arrival at Otu's dwelling, adjourned with his son to an outer court, and questioned him particularly as to the treatment of the missionaries. Little answer was made to these inquiries, but there seemed reason to suspect, not only that the king knew of the concealment of the men, on whose account the missionaries had been brought into this trouble, but that he had probably given some countenance to the recent treacherous attack of the natives.

At any rate, the seamen now appeared boldly among his attendants, and seemed to depend on his protection: and when Pomare insisted that these deserters should be forthwith delivered up, one of the sailors doggedly declared, that they should never take him on board the Nautilus alive.

CHAPTER VIII.

Missionaries resolve to leave the island. Conduct of Pomare. He revenges the injury of the missionaries. Departure for Port Jackson. Murder of Clode. Mr. Harris leaves Tahiti.

THE general body of the missionaries living at Matavai had, meanwhile, been apprised of the unexpected ill treatment of their brethren, by a boy whom one of them sent home shortly after the affray. They were thrown at once into the greatest consternation, and conceived their lives no longer safe, while they remained upon the island.

As soon as the other four returned in the evening, a consultation was held. Different views were of course entertained, in respect to the actual danger with which they were threatened. But from a great variety of reasons, a portion of them had by this time become tired of the undertaking, and on the following morning, eleven of their number hastily resolved that they would not stay longer on the island, but that they would instantly take advantage of the visit of the Nautilus, and return by her to their native country.

When this resolution of the missionaries came to be known throughout Tahiti, much regret was expressed by the natives. Pomare, who had both the most energy of character, and greatest influence of any in the island, acted on this occasion, in a manner that was almost noble.

Taking upon himself the whole obloquy of the insult offered to the strangers, by his erring countrymen, he, on the second day after the stripping of the missionaries, sent old Haamanemane, the priest, with a fowl, as an atonement, and a young plantain tree as a peace offering.

When he found that nothing would pacify the missionaries, he came himself to the settlement on the following day, expressing great sorrow at the resolution he had heard of, and using the most earnest entreaties to induce them to stay. The honourable chief even went to every room in the house, and to every berth where those were who had gone on board, and addressing every individual by name, begged of them not to go, giving them at the same time, every possible assurance of protection.

Nothing, however, could induce the eleven, who had originally taken the resolution, to remain another day at Tahiti. Yet were there six of the whole body, who still saw no sufficient reason to desert the work, which they had come so far to perform. The magnanimous resolution of these last gave great pleasure to Pomare, and many others on the island, who instantly set upon revenging the injury which the four missionaries had received.

Attacking the district in which the guilty natives resided, Pomare and his men killed two of them, before the departure of the eleven missionaries from the bay. Those who remained, resolving, however, to abstain entirely from war under any circumstances, sent what arms and ammunition they had, on board the Nautilus, excepting two muskets which they presented to Pomare and his wife.

They gave up also to this chief, in whom they resolved entirely to confide, their blacksmith's shop and all their tools; besides offering to put him in possession of the remainder of their property, which, however, he refused to take, except in the event of their leaving the island.

With respect to those who abandoned the mission, after a stormy and disagreeable passage of six weeks, they arrived at Port Jackson, and were received by the governor and chaplains of the settlement with every civility. It is not unworthy of notice here, that those eleven who fled to New South Wales, were ultimately exposed to greater dangers, and suffered, upon the whole, much more painful hardships, than those who bravely remained, to encounter whatever troubles might be attendant on the mission.

It appeared evident, also, from the improper conduct of several of them, after their arrival in the latter place, that the mission had rather been benefitted than the contrary, by the removal of men by no means calculated to uphold its character, or its religious efficiency. This, however, does not apply to those who were the greatest sufferers by this rash flight. One of them, named Mr. Hassel, was dangerously wounded, in New South Wales, by six ruffians, who broke into his lodgings, and, besides abusing his person, robbed him of almost every thing he possessed. Another was murdered under circumstances of barbarity, such as were little likely to have occurred even among the capricious islanders of the South Sea.

Mr. Clode, for that was the name of the latter unfortunate missionary, had lent a small sum of money to a man named Jones, who, with his wife, lived in a cottage a short distance from the town of Sydney. When Mr. Clode was preparing to sail to England, he asked this man to return the money, which, after some trouble, the other promised to do; appointing a certain day for the missionary to call at his house, when he would settle the business.

But, unwilling to return the money, the wretch, with his wife, planned the murder of the generous lender; who had been during all the time of his stay in the country, their greatest friend. Having got another accomplice, named Elbray, to assist in the murder, these monsters watched for the poor man's arrival. The wife took the children and some visitors out, and the two men made ready for the bloody deed, while the unsuspicious missionary sat down at a table to draw out a receipt.

While thus seated, Elbray went behind the victim with an axe in his hand, but, his heart failing him, he laid down his weapon and slipped out of the house. He had scarcely gone, however, when, standing without, he heard the first blow fall on the scull of the unhappy missionary.

The remainder of the tale is too horrible to relate, but after nearly severing the head from the body, one of the murderers carried it to a pit; and, covering it with boughs, they thought all was safe from discovery. Returning to the house, after this horrible deed, the wretches made themselves merry with their visitors, drinking and singing until the night was far advanced.

But the fate of the murderer may easily be anticipated, however well he imagines he has concealed his deed. Next morning a man, who laboured near the pit, was attracted towards it by curiosity upon observing the boughs; and removing them, he was shocked by the sight of a dead man's hand.

Running from the spot and giving the alarm, Jones and his wife immediately endeavoured to fasten the murder upon the poor man who had discovered the body. But blood having been traced from the very door of Jones's cottage to the pit, and other indisputable evidence having been found against him and his accomplices, the whole three were condemned to suffer for this atrocious murder.

They were executed on the spot where their house stood, it having by this time been razed to the ground by order of the Governor. The two men were hung in chains beside the pit, and the body of the woman was given to the surgeons for dissection.

To return to the missionaries now left at Tahiti. Though thus reduced in numbers, and all their efforts crippled and circumscribed, they did not seem discouraged, but rather determined to use renewed diligence. Nevertheless, the quarrel between Pomare and the people of an entire district on their account, threatened to involve the whole island in war.

Several circumstances arose out of this quar-

8

rel, which were of a very trying nature to Mr. Jefferson, and the others who had remained true to the mission. The occurrences which followed, between them and the natives, possess but little interest. Desertion among their own members added greatly to their troubles, and the unfortunate death of one of them, as it was supposed by the treachery of the natives, added much to their unhappiness.

The next thing that tended to the further weakening of the mission at Tahiti, was the departure of Mr. Harris, one of the few that remained, for New South Wales; an opportunity having offered by the arrival of the Betsey, an English letter of marque, in the bay, who, with a Spanish brig, her prize, was proceeding to Port Jackson.

This Mr. Harris was the same who has been so terrified by the islanders of Tongatabu; but having had the courage to remain at Tahiti, he now sought to pay a visit to Australia, promising to return when the Betsey should again visit these islands. The wish of the missionary having been agreed to, on the first day of the year

1800, the Betsey, with Mr. Harris on board, took her leave of the island of Tahiti.

CHAPTER IX.

Voyage of Mr. Ellis and his friends from England, to the Pacific. Arrival at New Zealand, and general impressions from the scenery and people. Anecdote of Tetoro. Arrival at Rapa, and general sketch. Thievish disposition of the natives. They attempt to steal the ship's dog. A chief jumps overboard with the cat. Arrival at Tabuai. Appearance of it, and of the natives. Arrival at Tahiti.

The interesting islands of the South Sea, not having been totally abandoned by the Society in London, in the year 1815, Mr. William Ellis, and Mr. Threlkeld, were appointed, not only to go to the Pacific as missionaries, but to make such researches in that region, as might help to guide the opinions, as to the future operations of the friends of missionary undertakings in England.

It was in the month of January, 1816, that these two missionaries and their families sailed from Portsmouth, for the Georgian and Society Islands in the South Sea. Touching at Madeira on their passage, their ship arrived in Rio Janeiro on the twentieth of March; and in this port they were detained for above six weeks.

Sailing thence by the eastern course, they passed the Cape of Good Hope, and it was not until the twenty-second of July, that their vessel cast anchor in Port Jackson, New South Wales. Here Mr. Ellis and his friend met with several of those missionaries who had been driven from Tahiti; and staying not less than five months on the Australian continent, in December, the same year, they again set sail in a brig called the Queen Charlotte, meaning to touch on their way to the Georgian Islands, at the celebrated island of New Zealand.

Arriving at New Zealand, the Queen Charlotte made for the Bay of Islands, where a missionary colony had already been planted, and where Mr. Ellis and his friends were greeted with much kindness. Here the strangers were gratified with a sight of the naked copper-coloured and highly tatooed native Zealanders; for they came off in numbers in their long canoes to the ship, anxious to sell to those on board, their fish and some curiosities of the island.

Making an excursion into the country afterwards, Mr. Ellis met with Tetoro, a chief, and a number of the islanders, who, on seeing the missionaries, ran forward to meet them, saying, 'how do you do?' as in England; but touching noses with the strangers, according to the custom of the country.

The chief was a tall fine looking man, about six feet high, and proportionably stout, his limbs firm and muscular; and when dressed in his war-cloak, with all his implements of death, he must have appeared formidable to his enemies. 'When acquainted with our business,' says Mr. Ellis, 'he prepared to accompany us; but before we set out, an incident occurred that greatly raised my estimation of his character. In front of the hut sat his wife, and around her were two or three little children playing. In passing from the hut to the boat, Tetoro struck one of the little ones with his foot; the child cried, and though the chief had his mat on and his gun in his hand, and was in the act of stepping into the boat where we were waiting for him, he no sooner heard its cries, than he turned back, took the child up in his arms, patted its little head, dried its tears, and giving it to the mother, hastened to join us. His conversation in the boat, during the remainder of the voyage, indicated no inferiority of intellect nor deficiency of information, as far as he possessed the means of obtaining it.'

The impression made upon the missionary by the sight of the forests in New Zealand, as he found them in their natural state upon the island, we cannot avoid also offering in his own words. 'We accompanied them' he says, 'to the adjacent forests. The earth was completely covered with thick, spreading, and forked roots, brambles, and creeping plants, overgrown with moss, and interwoven so as to form a kind of uneven matting, which rendered travelling exceedingly difficult. The underwood was in many parts thick, and the trunks of the lofty trees rose like

TETORO AND HIS CHILD.

Page 117.

clusters of pillars, supporting the canopy of interwoven boughs and verdant foliage, through which the sun's rays seldom penetrated.

'There were no trodden paths, and the wild and dreary solitude of the place was only broken by the voice of some lonely bird, which chirped among the branches of the bushes, or, startled by our intrusion on its retirement, darted across our path.

'A sensation of solemnity and awe involuntarily arose in the mind, while contemplating a scene of such peculiar character, so unlike the ordinary haunts of men, and so adapted, from the silent grandeur of his works, to elevate the soul with the sublimest conceptions of the Almighty. I was remarkably struck with the gigantic size of many of the trees, some of which appeared to rise nearly one hundred feet, without a branch, while two men with extended arms could not clasp their trunks.'

Such is the condition of the forests in New Zealand, so well described by this missionary, and making the face of the country so different from the romantic valleys and open glades which, with lofty mountains, diversify the scenery of the delightful island of Tahiti.

Some of the native chiefs, who had received a quantity of wheat from Mr. Marsden of New South Wales, about two years before, had sown it, and it had arrived to perfection; and the missionaries on the island having also tilled a field in the European manner, and sown wheat, Mr. Ellis found it growing green and flourishing when he visited the settlement.

This progress in agricultural art, with its labours and improvements, will doubtless extend among the New Zealanders, even to their native flax plant, which was also found growing strong and thickly in the low lands. Its long leaves or flags, shaped like a sword, furnish a fibre which makes a species of hemp. Of this the natives manufacture fishing-lines, twine, cordage, and even dresses, and it is expected to form an important article of commerce with New South Wales and England.

The population of New Zealand is much greater than that of the other smaller islands of the South Sea, being estimated at not less than half a million. The character of the inhabitants is now well known in Europe. They are possessed of much energy, both of body and mind, and discover none of the cowardice and effeminacy of the more gentle inhabitants of the Georgian Islands. Most of the warriors are about six feet in height, and strong and muscular in proportion. The whole people are hardy and industrious, but war is their delight.

They are much less superstitious than the other South Sea islanders, but they are more ferocious and sanguinary in their wars; and in cases of triumph over their enemies, their bloody vengeance and cruelty to their captives are truly horrible, and their cannibalism has been verified beyond a doubt.

So ferocious is their disposition, that no impression favourable to civilization has been made upon them, by the intercourse with a more humanized people, which the occasional visits of European ships have afforded them. On the contrary, they have been more ready to learn or to practise the vices of the Europeans than their virtues, as has been shown in several of their late atrocities.

Among such a people it may be supposed that little improvement is to be expected, merely from the mild and patient labours of missionaries, for a long period of time. Those, however, sent out by the church society in 1814, and now visited by Mr. Ellis in 1816, had not altogether laboured in vain. The general character of the people, in the neighbourhood of the settlement, appeared to the visitor to be improved.

Piety in some cases had been evinced; and the arts of civilized life had begun to attract the attention, and to employ the ingenuity of the natives. The wretched system of government in New Zealand, bringing with it, as it did, consequences continually tending to war and encouraging treachery and every species of disturbance of barbarity, formed the greatest obstacle to the Christianizing, or civilizing of the natives.

There is in fact no government, no general head over the people. The whole are under a subdivided and independent chieftainship, which occasions continual jealousies, quarrels, and bloodshed; and nurses the spirit of ferocity and savage cunning, which is inimical to the introduction of all virtue.

At the end of the year 1816, Mr. Ellis and his companion sailed from the Bay of Islands in New Zealand; and on the twenty-sixth of January, 1817, at day-break in the morning, they discovered themselves to be close to an island called Rapa, which had been discovered by Vancouver in 1791. The appearance of this island from the sea, like that of most in the Pacific ocean, seems to be singularly romantic.

No low land met the sea on its shores, but lofty mountains rising towards its centre, were washed at their bases by the restless waves; while a part of the banks, covered with bushes and verdure, surrounded them, like belts, and winding valleys between shot farther than the eye could reach, into the interior of the country.

The noble mountains, which form the high land in the centre of the island, are so singularly broken in shape, as to resemble, in no small degree, a range of irregularly inclined cones, or cylindrical columns, which their original discoverer supposed to be towers, or fortifications, manned with natives.

Sailing round this picturesque island and admiring its scenery, the missionaries observed several canoes put off from the shore. About thirty of them soon after surrounded the ship, but kept for a long time at a considerable distance; the natives seeming to look at the European vessel with much surprise and emotion.

The bodies of these islanders were finely formed, their features regular, and in many cases handsome. Their countenances were partly shaded with black curling, and sometimes long straight hair; and their skin, not tattooed like the New Zealanders, was of a dark copper colour. A girdle of yellow leaves, round their waists, was all the covering they wore.

After some difficulty, the missionaries got a few of them to approach the ship's side, and one of them to accept some hooks for a lobster which was perceived lying at the bottom of his boat. The chief, after gazing curiously at the hooks, gave them to a boy, who, having no pocket or place about his person to put them in, thrust them into his mouth.

When the missionary offered his hand to the savage chief to assist him in getting into the ship, the latter, first drawing back, afterwards put the white hand close to his nose and smelt at it, as if to ascertain what sort of being he was thus coming in contact with. When he had at length climbed up the ship's side and got on the quarter deck, the Captain politely handed him a chair and made signs for him to sit, but after examining the seat, he put it aside and sat down on the deck.

Although these islanders were shy at first, they soon became as bold in their manners as they are described to be savage in their looks. Many of them began to climb over the bulwarks of the vessel, and soon crowds of them appeared on the deck. The object of the fiercest looking seemed to be, to carry off whatever they took a fancy to, and that either by stealth or force ; so while the others were gazing about, a gigantic fellow catching hold of one of the ship-boys, endeavoured to lift him from the deck, but the lad, struggling, got free from his grasp.

He next seized the cabin-boy, but the sailors interfered, and when the savage found himself prevented from carrying the boy off, he pulled the youth's woolen shirt over his head, with which he prepared to leap overboard, when the sailors arrested him, and made him give it up.

Another native seized a large ship-dog, which was on board, and the animal, being terrified by the appearance of the islanders, lost all his courage, and suffered himself to be taken up in the arms of the man, who was proceeding with it over the ship's side, when the chain by which it was bound to its kennel prevented him. The savage then tried to carry off kennel and all, but finding it made fast to the deck, he was obliged to relinquish it, and seemed much disappointed.

While the natives gazed round them for something else that they could capture, a young cat, which had been brought from Port Jackson, made its appearance from the cabin gangway. The moment the unconscious animal came upon deck, a native sprang upon it like a tiger, and, catching it up, jumped overboard with it, and plunged into the sea. Those on board immediately ran to the side, to see what the savage meant to do with the cat.

He had now risen to the surface, and was swimming vigorously towards a canoe, which lay about fifty yards off. When he got to the canoe he held up the cat in both his hands, over his head, in the highest exultation, while the natives were paddling in every direction towards him, to get a sight of the strange creature which he had brought from the ship.

When the Captain observed the success of the robber, he levelled his musket, and was about to fire at the man, had he not been withheld by the arguments of the missionaries. He then gave orders to clear the ship ; and a strange scene ensued, for there was a sudden scuffle between the sailors and the natives.

Many of the latter were at once pitched overboard by the sailors, which was not the slightest inconvenience to them, while others clambered up the shrouds, and hung about the chains. The dog, formerly so terrified, now sought revenge, by tearing the legs of some natives who would not leave the ship, while others required the long knives carried by seamen in sailing the South Sea to be used, before they were completely expelled.

The inhabitants of Rapa, in most particulars, bear a general resemblance to the other islanders of the Pacific Ocean ; but are much less civilized in their manners, more rude in their arts, and possess, consequently, fewer comforts than the Tahitians, or any other natives of the more northern islands.

Upon being afterwards visited by other missionaries, Rapa was found to contain about two thousand inhabitants ; and, savage as they are, considerable improvement has been since effected among them. The island itself is about twenty miles in circumference, has an excellent harbour, though with an intricate entrance ; and is tolerably well wooded and watered.

Leaving Rapa, and sailing northerly, the missionaries, on the third of February, descried the island of Tabuai, which had originally been discovered by Cook, in the year 1777. This was the first of the South Sea islands which was seen by the missionaries in the Duff, in 1797; and here, also, the mutineers who rose against their officers, whom they expelled from their ship, the Bounty, in 1789, found their first refuge.

The island of Tabuai is less picturesque than Rapa, but is hilly and verdant. Some of the hills had, to our visitors' apprehension, a sunburnt appearance, unlike what is usual in the other islands, but others were partially covered with wood.

A reef of coral runs out into the sea which surrounds it, protecting the lowlands from the incursion of its waves. As the ship approached the shore, a number of canoes filled with natives, came out and surrounded the strangers.

These canoes were sixteen to twenty feet long, resembling those they had seen at Rapa, but less noble in form than the prowed boats of the New Zealanders. The lower part was formed of the hollow trunk of a tree, and the sides, stem and stern, were composed of thin planks,

9

sewed together, with a sort of twine made from the fibrous husk of the cocoa nut.

A fine looking chief came on board the ship with the other natives, and did all in his power to induce the ship's people to land on his island. This request was, however, refused for the present, at least; and as the islander staid on board the whole of that day and night, he was considerably affected by the motion of the vessel.

The missionary describes the manners of this man to have been mild and friendly, and was much struck with his handsome form and noble mien. His only dress was a broad girdle round his loins, his body being but little tatooed, and his glossy black hair tied in a bunch on the crown of his head, while its extremities hung in ringlets over his shoulders. Next morning a party from the ship going on shore, found the people friendly, though not numerous, and quite ready to barter their fowls and island fruits, for the fish hooks and other articles of cutlery which the ship had brought.

When a more extended view of the natives was obtained, the strangers found many who wore, besides a light robe of their native cloth over their shoulders, folds of white or yellow cloth bound round their heads, which gave them, of course, much of an Asiatic appearance. Many also had round their necks, strings of a strong scented nut called the pandanus, the smell of which is, by use, grateful to the islanders of the Pacific.

Sailing from Tabuai, on the fourth of February, unfavourable winds retarded their progress, so that it was not until the tenth, that the missionaries were gratified with their first sight of the celebrated island of Tahiti. About sunset, their ship drew near to Point Venus, which they descried to the south, and sailing along, charmed with the rich and varied scenery of this island paradise, several canoes of the natives came out to meet them. Being, however, drifted off shore in the night, it was not until mid-day of the sixteenth of February 1817, that their ship cast anchor in Matavai bay.

CHAPTER X.

Impressions of the Scenery of Tahiti. Landing of a Horse, and astonishment of the natives. Visit of the Queen and her attendants to the ship. Departure for Eimeo, and arrival there. State of the Mission, and Sketch of late Changes in these Islands. Conversion of Pomare. Abolition of Idolatry.

THE effect produced by the scenery of the island of Tahiti upon Mr. Ellis and his friends, as their ship first sailed into Matavai Bay, within which the other missionaries had formerly dwelt, is scarcely to be described. The sea, on which they glided along, was smooth and glassy; the morning was fair, and the climate already gave an exhilaration to the spirits; a light breeze wafted along the shore, while the sky above their heads was without a cloud.

All that our missionary had ever heard of this most enchanting island, seemed surpassed by the reality, when its romantic scenery came fairly before his eyes. He speaks of beholding successively 'all the diversity of hill and valley, broken or stupendous mountains and rocky precipices, clothed with every variety of verdure, from the moss of the jutting promontories on the shores, to the deep and rich foliage of the bread-fruit tree; the oriental luxury of the tropical pandanus, or the waving plumes of the lofty and graceful cocoa-nut grove.'

We have already given some description of this bay, as it impressed Captain Wilson and his friends; but to the imaginative eye of the present missionary traveller, it had charms of a still higher order. The cataract rushing down the mountain side,—the clear stream stealing through the beautiful valleys,—the numerous hills and mountains towering in the back ground; while in front, the green slopes which sweep down from the groves among the hills, are met 'by the white-crested waters of the Pacific, rolling their waves of foam in splendid majesty upon the coral reefs; or dashing in spray against its broken shore,'—all formed a scene of which language can very inadequately convey an idea. Buried among the valleys, or peeping out from the groves of fruit trees, the houses of the natives are here and there seen, to give life, as well as the idea of enjoyed happiness, to this delicious Eden of the South Sea.

The missionaries regarded the natives, who had by this time crowded on board, with much interest, as those among whom the rest of their days might probably be spent. But in stopping at Matavai Bay, they were but paying a visit to Tahiti; for they were, in the first instance, bound for the neighbouring island of Eimeo, whither, it will be remembered, the original missionaries had fled with the king, after they were forced to leave the former island, several years before. King Pomare had, however, before the present visit of Mr. Ellis, returned to Tahiti, although none of the old missionaries had, as yet, accompanied him; a remarkable revolution having in the meantime taken place. His Tahitian Majesty soon came on board, and welcomed Mr. Ellis, having sent before him his present of provisions.

Pomare II. was about forty years of age, and his tall, and almost gigantic figure, his kingly appearance, his oriental features and copper colour, and his dress of white native cloth contrasting with his glossy black hair, impressed the missionary with involuntary respect.

He spoke a little English, and inquired of the missionaries concerning King George of Britain; asking also some questions about the time of the departure of their ship, and what had been the incidents of their voyage. He brought with him a small English Bible, out of which Mr. Ellis, at his request, read him two chapters, he being at this time able to understand the English language in some measure, though little able to speak it.

Ascending from the ship's cabin, and going to see what things had been brought from New Holland, his Tahitian Majesty was highly delighted with a horse which had been sent to him as a present; it being an animal unknown in the islands of the South Seas. It was intended to send the horse ashore at once, for which purpose the king ordered a pair of large canoes to the ship's side. The animal was then hoisted out of the hold on slings, and from the deck hauled by ropes to the yard arm, in order to be from thence dropped upon the platform laid across the two canoes.

While, however, the beast was hoisted up, and hung by the middle from the yard arm in the air; to the great consternation of the king and the other natives, some of the bandages round it gave way. By this accident it was left suspended by the neck and fore legs; and after sprawling in that situation for some time, slipped through the slings and plunged into the sea.

The natives looked on in astonishment, until they perceived the animal rise to the surface, and after snorting and shaking its head, begin to swim vigorously towards the shore. They then jumped into the sea after him; and followed him like a shoal of sharks, some seizing him by the tail, others by his mane, until the poor beast was terrified almost into drowning. The king shouted as loud as he could, calling upon his people to leave the horse; but the clamour and noise prevented him from being heard, and though the Captain of the ship lowered down the boat for the same purpose, it was of no avail.

At length the exhausted animal reached the

shore in safety. When he got out of the water, and began to walk along the beach, the natives, perceiving that he was not a fish, fled with precipitation from so strange a quadruped; some climbing trees to be enabled to get a sight of him in safety, and others crouching behind the rocks and bushes by the shore, while he passed.

To them the poor horse was a sight equally astonishing and alarming. But when they observed one of the seamen, who had been sent after the beast, approach it without fear, and take hold of the halter still hanging by its neck, to lead it along, they began to gather round to satisfy their curiosity.

The queen soon after this, paid the missionary a visit on board. Mr. Ellis describes her as in stature about the middle size, extremely elegant in form, and prepossessing in her whole appearance, her complexion fairer than any of the natives he had yet seen. He thought her voice somewhat harsh, and her manners less engaging than those of some of her companions. Her dress was flowing and tastefully arranged, being of native cloth, beautifully white; it was formed like the Roman toga, fastened to her left shoulder, and hung down to her ankle. Her hair was somewhat fair, and she wore on her head a bonnet, made of green and yellow cocoa-nut leaves.

She had no rings in her ears, but in the perforations of each, were inserted some flowers from a fragrant plant called the Cape Jessamin. Her sister, named Pomare Vahine, accompanied her to the ship, as did also her daughter, who appeared about six years of age, and who with her nurse and other attendants was brought into the ship's cabin. A numerous retinue followed these personages, and after spending two hours on board the vessel, unable however to address a word to the Captain or the missionary, the whole, after receiving a few presents, took their departure, and in many canoes, returned to the shore.

But the greatest diversion the natives had, was with the horse, which had been left for the first night tied up, and under the charge of one of the most favourite of the king's chiefs. On the next morning, it was led out, while the mul-

THE NATIVES AND THE HORSE.

Page 140.

titude gathered around, and gazed upon it with pleasure and astonishment.

The king had also come down to the beach; and a saddle and bridle having been brought and delivered to his majesty, he begged that the animal might be invested with them, and that some one might be placed on his back. The horse's accoutrements being accordingly put on, the Captain of the ship mounted him, and rode along the beach. Upon which the natives shouted with delight, calling the animal in their language, a land-running pig, a man-carrying pig, and other names expressive of their ideas of such a wonderful creature.

The horse being left in the king's possession, and all things settled that were intended for the present to be done in Tahiti, the ship next day weighed anchor, and soon arrived at Eimeo, which is only about fourteen miles distant from the former island. Eimeo, or as it was formerly called Moorea, is twenty-five miles in circumference, and fully as beautiful and romantic in its scenery as Tahiti itself.

A coral reef surrounds it like a ring, extending

in some places above a mile from the shore, and on this beautiful circle, over which the sea constantly froths and washes, several small and verdant islands rise green and romantic. This island was a favourite retreat of the king of Tahiti; and was now the head quarters of that mission to the South Sea, which amidst every discouragement had never been wholly removed or abandoned.

The ship soon entered the grand harbour of Taloo, whose romantic scenery and awful solitude made the deepest impression on his European visitors. Although the mountains round this bay are very precipitous and abrupt, and are in many parts wooded almost to the summit, they are not so lofty as the highest mountain in Tahiti; and the streams that rush from their cliffs, and wind down the valleys, are more like mountain torrents than rivers.

Beyond the first range of mountains, and in the interior of the island, is a large and beautiful lake, which is well stocked with fish, besides being a great resort for wild ducks, that are often taken in great numbers on its bosom. This lake is called Tamai, and a sequestered native village, of the same name, sits quietly and hermit-like on its verdant margin.

Mr. Ellis was soon enabled to go on shore at Eimeo, where he was greeted by the four missionaries now on the island, (as well as by several of the chiefs, who had also heard of his arrival,) with a cordial and most encouraging welcome. But during the time he was on his long passage, or rather before his leaving Europe, a religious revolution had taken place in these islands; so unexpected, and so effectual, that the account he now obtained of it, for the first time, filled him with a pleasing astonishment.

In short, Pomare, the king, from whom he had just parted, had, with several of the principal chiefs, been converted to Christianity; idolatry had been publicly abolished; and, both in respect of religion and civilization, the way had been cleared, within a few short years, for those remarkable proceedings which have since taken place among the islands of the South Sea.

Before the expiration of the year 1814, the small number of missionaries now labouring in

Eimeo, were attended by about three hundred scholars. Upwards of two hundred grown persons had given in their names as professors of christianity, and the reformation had made its way with extraordinary success into the neighbouring islands of Huahine, Raiatea, and Sir Charles Sanders' island, besides the effects produced in the larger island of Tahiti.

In the year 1815, a pleasing example was furnished, at a public entertainment in Eimeo, of the effects of this extensive reformation in the islands of the South Sea. Pomare Vahine, daughter of the king of Raiatea, and sister of the queen of Tahiti, wife of Pomare, having paid a visit to this island, on her way to Tahiti, where she was going to see her sister,—a grand entertainment was prepared for her by the native chiefs of Eimeo. A large quantity of food of different kinds having been dressed, it was usual that it should first be offered to the idols, as mentioned in the former case with Pomare.

While the people looked on, expecting the priests to select the offering, one of Vahine's attendants, being a convert to Christianity, came forward, and uncovering his head, in an audible voice, addressed the God of Heaven with thanksgiving and acknowledgment for this food.

The multitude witnessed this scene with astonishment; but no opposition was offered, and the food being now considered as offered to the God of the missionaries, and not to their own idols, no one dared to suggest an alteration, and the stranger lady acquiesced in the bold measure of her attendant.

CHAPTER XI.

Mr. Ellis sails to the district of Afaraitu. A Tahitian dinner. The valleys of Afaraitu. Forming of a Missionary Station there, and setting up of a Printing Press. Astonishment and crowding of the Natives at the first working of the Press. Printing and Book-binding. Eagerness of the People for books. Effects of the Introduction of Christianity.

It was while matters were in this state, and even more advanced than we have yet related, that Mr. Ellis landed in the island of Eimeo. In the course of the first week of his stay amongst his brethren, he made several excursions into the interior of the district. He found the soil, in the level parts of the valleys in particular, to consist of a rich vegetable mould. He also saw several plantations well stocked with the various productions of the island, but want of cultivation had rendered some portion of the lowland, rank with its own luxuriance, and thickly covered with long grass and brushwood.

He next accompanied one of the missionaries

on a canoe voyage to another district of the island, lying about twenty miles distant from the settlement. Two natives paddled their canoe, and they skimmed lightly along the smooth water that lay within the coral reef before mentioned. When they had reached a place called Moru, they landed and visited a friendly chief, who, as usual, set before them an abundant refreshment, which, being served up in the true Tahitian style, and the first native meal our traveller had eaten on the island, he observed very minutely how it was conducted.

'When the food was ready,' he says, 'we were requested to seat ourselves on the dry grass, that covered the floor of the house. A number of the broad leaves of the purau, having the stalks plucked off close to the leaf, were then spread on the ground, in two or three successive layers, with the downy or under side upwards, and two or three were handed by a servant to each individual, instead of a plate. By the side of these vegetable plates, a small cocoanut shell of salt water was placed for each person. Large quantities of fine large bread-fruit, roasted on hot stones, were now brought in, and a number of fish that had been wrapped in plantain leaves, and broiled on the embers, were placed beside them.

'A bread-fruit and a fish was handed to each individual, and, having implored a blessing, we began to eat, dipping every mouthful of bread-fruit, or fish, into the small vessel of salt water, without which, it would, to the natives, have been unsavoury and tasteless. I opened the leaves, found the fish nearly broiled, and, imitating the practice of those around me, dipped several of the first pieces I took into the dish placed by my side: but there was a bitterness in the sea water which rendered it rather unpalatable; I therefore dispensed with the further use of it, and finished my meal with the bread-fruit and fish.'

Resuming their journey about two in the afternoon, the missionaries came about sun-set to the district called Afaraitu, which is on the eastern side of the island, and lies opposite to the district of Aheturu in the island of Tahiti. This beautiful spot, which became afterwards an important missionary station, seems to have been very populous. On examining the district next morning, they were delighted with its fertility, extent, and resources. It is described as comprising two valleys, or rather one large valley partially divided by a narrow hilly ridge, extending from the mountains in the interior, towards the shore.

The same fertility, richness, and luxuriant verdure, found in the finest portions of this and the other islands, were abundantly displayed here; trees and shrubberies rising green and variegated to the very summits of the mountains. 'Several broad cascades,' says Mr. Ellis, 'flowed in silver streams down the sides of the mountains, and, broken occasionally by a jutting rock, presented their sparkly waters in beautiful contrast with the rich and dark foliage of the stately trees, and the flowering shrubs that bordered their course.'

Not to dwell upon the further description of this charming district, the missionaries soon saw its advantages for a second settlement. The land between the shore and the mountains was not swampy and luxuriant only, like some other parts, but high, healthy, and beautiful.

Added to this, was an abundance of the productions of nature all around; and a sweet and convenient stream of water wound down the valley, and discharged itself into the sea at the bottom of the little bay. The exploring missionaries, perceiving all these advantages for their proposed settlement, lost no time in waiting on the principal chiefs of the neighbourhood upon the business, who were quite pleased, and promised every assistance in the erection of the necessary houses.

By this time, the progress of the reformation in the islands was so extensive, that our travellers were only restrained from forming new settlements, and prosecuting new plans with regard to the other islands, by the smallness of their present number, and the want of hands to finish their vessels. Mr. Ellis having, however, brought with him a printing press and types from the mother country, and having himself learned the art of printing while in England, at the request of the directors of the London Society, it was soon decided by the missionaries, that they should have their printing press set up in this newly surveyed district of Afaraitu, as soon as they could erect a suitable building.

In this work, King Pomare, now at Tahiti, took a most cordial and decided interest. He wrote a letter to the chief of the district, requesting him zealously to assist the missionaries in their undertaking; and in a few weeks came himself to the island, in order to hasten forward the work. Different parties of the natives were, for this purpose, formed by his direction. One attended to the building of the printing office, and another laboured at the erection of a house for Mr. Ellis.

These houses were built of wood, in the manner usual in this island. The sides were formed by upright posts, about three feet apart, the interstices filled up with a wattled matting, and in some places left quite open; while rafters and cross beams upheld the roof, which was formed of leaves and very ingeniously wrought over a matting.

A wall, or well formed paling, usually surrounds the houses, leaving a court of considerable extent, which is often paved with black or party-coloured pebble stones, and is usually kept smooth and clean. When the printing office was nearly complete, the missionaries finished it, not only by making a floor, and boarding the sides of the house; but by placing in it two or three windows of glass, much to the admiration of the natives.

But the printing press was the great object of the admiring curiosity of these people. The fame of this wonderful machine had spread over all Eimeo, and also several of the neighbouring islands. Large numbers of the people, from all parts round, flocked to the spot, as well as to get a sight of it, as to attend the religious instructions of the missionaries. It was not more than three months after Mr. Ellis and his friends had paid their first visit to Afaraitu, before the house was ready, and the press set up. The king having been informed of the fact, by his own desire he came, accompanied by a body of his favourite chiefs, and followed by a large concourse of people, to witness the first operations of the famous machine.

He entered the building with his chiefs only, but the windows of it required to be screened, to prevent the annoyance of the eager multitude. It was proposed that the king should put together the first letters with his own hand. The composing stick was given to him for this purpose, and never did a king feel so proud of being a printer. By the direction of Mr. Ellis, he filled the stick out of the boxes, with the large letters of the alphabet; for they were now about setting up the first sheet of a spelling-book.

As he knew the alphabet, he next set in order the small letters, and when the first page was finished, he looked with wonder upon the effects of his own talents at printing. The others having, while the king looked on, put together sufficient matter to make a form, on one side of a sheet, he was next ordered to ink the types.

He took the ink balls from Mr. Ellis, and struck the face of the letters three times. This was a feat; but what was next to be done? The sheet was laid on the parchment, and covered down over the types. The king was directed to pull the handle of the press; he pulled it vigorously; and when the covering was lifted up, the chiefs and attendants pressed forward to see what their monarch had effected.

When they beheld the letters black, newly impressed, and well defined, there was a general expression of wonder and delight. His Majesty repeated the act; and now, showing one of the sheets to the crowd without, when they saw what he had produced from this marvellous machine, 'they raised,' as we are told, 'one general shout of astonishment and joy.' He continued, as well as the crowd, to watch the progress of printing, the whole of the day, and, for several days after this, paid much attention to the process so interesting to all.

A spelling-book in the Tahitian language being most needed, this was the first volume printed on the island. The king in the course of his studies in this new art, was engaged in counting several of the letters as they were used; and evinced much surprise at finding, that in sixteen pages of the spelling-book, the letter *a* was used above five thousand times. A Tahitian catechism was the next book printed, of which between two and three thousand were thrown off; and, next after this, a translation of St. Luke's Gospel.

Before the first sheet of this latter work was printed, a new arrival from England gladdened the labourers in this work. The brig Active brought an accession to their strength, of not less than six new missionaries, at the very time when they were most required. The same vessel brought also a supply of printing paper, sent by the Bible Society, than which hardly any thing could have been more seasonable.

Mr. Crook, who it will be remembered was the missionary that, several years before, was left alone upon one of the Marquesan islands, gave Mr. Ellis the 'greatest assistance in this work. Having instructed two of the natives to perform the more laborious parts, particularly the working of the press, these men soon became good workmen, and received regular wages for their business.

The curiosity of the natives to see this machine, that made 'the speaking paper,' was unbounded. None but the king and chiefs were admitted with the workmen into the building; but the crowd without was immense, and increased as the work proceeded. The printing press became a matter of universal conversation, and great multitudes came from the adjacent islands, and all the neighbouring districts, to catch a glimpse of any thing connected with this astonishing machine.

The excitement manifested, says Mr. Ellis, 'frequently resembled that with which the people of England would hasten to witness, for the first time, the ascent of a balloon, or the movement of a steam carriage.' 'So great,' he adds, 'was the influx of strangers, that for several weeks before the first portion of the Scriptures was finished, the district of Afaraitu resembled a public fair. The beach was lined with canoes from distant parts of Eimeo and other islands; the houses of the inhabitants were thronged, and small parties had erected their temporary encampments in every direction. The school, during the week, and chapel on the sabbath, though capable of containing six hundred persons, were found too small for those who sought admittance.'

Those who got near enough, peeped through every crevice of the building, for the windows could hardly be got at, in order to obtain a sight of the press, and the marvellous work that was going on; whilst involuntary exclamations were often heard from them, in their admiration of British skill and knowledge.

'The printing-office,' continues Mr. Ellis, 'was daily crowded by the strangers, who thronged the doors, in such numbers, as to climb upon each other's backs, or on the sides of the windows, so as frequently to darken the place. The house had been inclosed with a fence five or six feet high; but this, instead of presenting an obstacle to the gratification of their curiosity, was converted into a means of facilitating it; numbers were constantly seen sitting on the top of the railing, whereby they were able to look over the heads of their companions who were round the windows.'

Some strangers having come to Eimeo, all the

way from the pearl islands, a small cluster of little more than coral rocks, lying at a considerable distance north-east of Tahiti, had the address to get among the king's train, and were by him hospitably treated with a near inspection of the press.

When admitted into the printing-office, and when they beheld the machine worked by a native printer, their surprise and astonishment were truly affecting. It was some time before they would approach very near, and appeared at a loss whether to consider it an animal or a machine.

Mr. Ellis was able to converse with these strangers, who informed him that they also had abandoned the worship of idols, which they said were only evil spirits who had done them no good. They too, as well as the other tribes who waited without, expressed the most eager desire to be supplied with the spelling-books and scriptures, which the missionaries were printing.

Having brought out with them to these islands the presses used by bookbinders also, they now set them up, and prepared to bind the books that they had printed. This process, when commenced, was a new object of wonder to the natives. A copy of the spelling-book they had half-bound in red morocco, which, as the first fruits of their labours, they presented to the king; and his satisfaction at this, as his Majesty was now somewhat of a learned person, was evidently very great.

Next, the queen and chiefs were supplied; but the demand was so great, that some circumspection was necessary in the distribution of the means of knowledge. The materials for binding books, which had been brought from England, were soon exhausted. The native cloth however, which is made from the bark of a tree, was made to supply the deficiency; and this being laid together in many folds, and pressed, became a tolerably good substitute for leather.

Some of the natives, having quickly learned the art of binding books in their simple manner, were now overwhelmed with business, and found their new calling very profitable. So great, however, was the number of people to be supplied, that parties of natives, who had come in their canoes from the neighbouring islands, solely for the purpose of procuring copies of the spelling-books, or gospel, often waited five or six weeks for them, rather than go away without.

Sometimes these simple people came with bundles of letters from their friends, ordering 'the word of Luke,' or other books; the letters being written on the plantain leaf, which was rolled up like a scroll, and may have appeared like the ancient papyrus of the Jews or Egyptians.

The spelling books and similar works had been hitherto distributed gratuituously among the people; but when Luke's Gospel was printed, it was thought expedient to take a price for the book, which was generally paid in cocoa-nut oil. It was most affecting, we are told, to see the eagerness with which these poor islanders came from afar, in their light canoes, for gospel books.

As they drew near the shore, where the missionary house stood, if any one appeared in sight to receive them, their practice was to hold up their hands simultaneously, carrying the bamboo canes filled with cocoa-nut oil, and to shout *Te parua na Luka,* that is, The word of Luke; while they showed, triumphantly, that they had the means of paying for it.

'Often,' says Mr. Ellis, 'when standing at my door, which was but a short distance from the sea-beach, as I have gazed on the varied beauties of the rich and glowing landscape, and the truly picturesque appearance of the island of Tahiti, fourteen or eighteen miles distant, the scene has been enlivened by the light and nautilus-like sail of the buoyant canoes;' seen in all the different degrees of size and distinctness as they floated on the shining bosom of the waters; till they came skimming along within the little bay, and lowered their sail, and set up their shout for that word of divine truth, which was now made known in the charming isles of the Pacific ocean.

Previous to this time, and in consequence of the religious revolution in these islands, a change had been effected in the state of domestic society, which is so interesting as to deserve particular observation here. It had been one of the rules of their idolatry, and was in consequence a sacred and inviolate custom in all the Georgian islands, that the females of any household should not eat with the males ; nor were they even allowed to cook their victuals at the same fire with the men, nor yet keep their food in the same place appointed for the males.

The poor females, all over these islands, prepared and eat their victuals in lonely solitude, and thus all parties lost that comfort and pleasure, which is enjoyed by family meetings at the social meal.

Many circumstances grew out of this cruel arrangement, extremely painful to reflect upon, and degrading to the females, considering the means of enjoyment which these delightful islands afforded. But all this was changed by the happy event, of the propagation of the mild and elevating principles of christianity, in these islands, which had hitherto been literally the habitations of horrid cruelty.

The idols Oro and Tane, to whom so many public and private immolations had been made, both of human life, of happiness, and of peace, had no sooner been publicly burned in Tahiti, as before stated, than the wife was restored to the full society of her husband. The daughter could eat and drink in her father's presence. Domestic comfort and intercourse were every where promoted, and parents and children could rejoice together in the unspeakable blessings of a humane religion.

CHAPTER XII.

Missionary vessel built at Eimeo. The launch. Voyage of Mr. Ellis to Raiatea. Hospitality of the natives. Description of a district of Raiatea. Ruins of an idol temple. Natural Fort. Arrival at the missionary station. Examination of the school. Dinner in the grove.

Before we proceed to follow Mr. Ellis in his farther travels and voyages among these islands, it may be proper to mention, that, when he arrived first in Eimeo, he found the other missionaries engaged in building a vessel of their own,

11

which should serve them in their excursions among the islands, or go, if needful, as far as Port Jackson.

In this plan, Pomare, the king, cordially joined; even finding the materials, as far as the islands could supply them, and giving otherwise much assistance. It was not, however, until the arrival of the new missionaries, that there were hands enough to finish it; but then it was soon completed, and on the seventh of December, 1817, it was intended to be launched.

On the day appointed, crowds were gathered from all quarters to witness the launching and the naming of so great a vessel; for the ship was of seventy tons' burden, and the king himself was to name her in form and manner such as the natives had never witnessed.

All things being ready, and strong ropes passed round the vessel, by which she was to be hauled forward into the water, the wedges were knocked away by the carpenters, but still the vessel did not move. The king, who stood in readiness with a bottle of wine in his hand, shouted to the natives to pull away, while one of his orators, or bards, who was perched upon a rock near, sang a launching song with great emphasis. The natives pulled and the man sung and shouted, but still the vessel moved not over the rollers, along which she should have slid into the sea.

At length, as they persevered in hauling, she began to move, and seemed steadily riding forth to meet the wave, amid the shouts of the delighted people. Pomare had been stationed at the edge of the beach, and just as the ship was entering the water, he threw the bottle of wine at her bows, pronouncing her name, and wishing her prosperity, in an audible voice.

This operation, the breaking of the bottle, the spilling of the wine, and the scattering of the pieces of broken glass, so astonished the islanders who were on the side where it was done, that ceasing suddenly, they stood and gazed, while those on the contrary side continued to pull; when, in an instant, the vessel heeled over and fell on her beam-ends, to the great consternation of the shouting multitude.

This was a sad disaster, for it destroyed the

eclat of the launch, and greatly damped the spirits, for a time, of all concerned. However, every effort was employed to set her up again, and by exerting their united strength, by the afternoon of the same day she was quite righted, and the Pacific received, at length, the missionary ship, amidst the shouts of the multitude, who clad the shores of the bay.

It was in this vessel that Mr. Ellis and his companions, with their baggage, were carried to their new station at Huahine. Soon after, having completed the necessary buildings in this island, he proposed to pay a visit to the island of Raiatea, where a missionary station had been placed sometime before.

This island was not more than thirty miles distant from Huahine, and setting sail one morning at nine o'clock, the missionary expected to reach it long before the evening. The promising morning turned soon, however, into a lowering day.

A boisterous and threatening wind arose, which continuing the whole of the day, their passage in the small boat was both disagreeable and danger-

THE LAUNCH.

Page 169.

ous. The storm had long hid all the shores around from their view, and it was near midnight before they again made the land, which fortunately turned out to be one part of Raiatea, to which they were bound.

Having at length landed on the beach, weary and drenched, they found some houses of the natives, where the people readily roused themselves to entertain and comfort them. Having rested for the night, the travellers went out to view that part of the island on which they had happened to land.

They found this district of Raiatea remarkably well cultivated, the land being rich and good; large gardens had been formed by the natives, and were well stocked with the most valuable roots and vegetables, indigenous to these islands. This was, in fact, a place of celebrity in the whole neighbourhood, particularly, from its being the spot where one of the most remarkable marais, or temples, for idol worship, was situated.

When Mr. Ellis and his friend came to view this temple, they found its ruins like those of that one in Tahiti. But the sacrifices to the god

Oro, which had taken place here, seem to have been more sanguinary than usual; for the spot was surrounded with human as well other bones, lying scattered around in heaps.

To their great horror, the missionaries also found a large enclosure, the walls of which were formed entirely of human skulls. These had principally or entirely belonged to those who were slain in battle; for the natives were not so cruel at any time as to offer living sacrifices to their idols, or to kill men before them. Like all similar erections, this idol temple was situated in the midst of a grove of beautiful trees.

This small, but picturesque island, is, though longer, not unlike the celebrated rock of Gibralter; a lofty natural fort, rising in the interior near the one end, which the natives resort to in seasons of war. This peculiar rock is called by the natives a *pare*, and it was here that, the Tahitian resisted all the power of King Pomare, aided by the skill of Captain Bishop and twenty-four other Englishmen, who had brought with them a brass four pounder. This single small cannon was never used, being only like a popgun, when brought before this magnificent and commanding rock.

Departing from this district in the afternoon, the travellers enjoyed a pleasant sail within the reef, along the eastern shore, on their way to the missionary station at the other end of the island. The scenery they passed was rich and romantic as usual; and the cordial welcome of their friends and fellow labourers, made their voyage terminate delightfully. The state of the mission and of the schools for teaching the natives, were such as to be extremely satisfactory to the visitors.

In addition to learning to read and spell in their own tongue, the natives had been taught to sing translations of many psalms and hymns, to which the tunes used in England had been fitted, in a very pleasing and melodious manner. To hear the simple natives of the South Sea chanting the solemn melody of the old hundredth psalm, or warbling the soul of music and of pathos in the hymn of the Sicilian mariners, must certainly have been singularly affecting.

The annual exminations of these schools was, as Mr. Ellis says, a festivity most exhilarating and interesting. They were held in the chapel of the station, and were closed by an entertainment provided by the chiefs, for the whole of the children, on a rising ground, in the vicinity of the governor's house.

Here, being followed by the multitude of their parents and friends, with the teachers, not less than three hundred boys, and two hundred girls, sat down on the grass, to a plentiful repast, on the occasion when Mr. Ellis was present. In the centre, between the rows of boys and girls, tables were spread for the chiefs, as well as for the parents and friends of the children, in the style and manner of out-door festivity in England.

The food was carved, and handed to the children, who sat on the grass on either side, headed by their teachers. Who could have supposed, in Captain Cook's time, that such a spectacle as this would have been witnessed in the islands of the South Sea?

A short address from Mr. Ellis closed the entertainment; after which the whole stood up around, and sung a hymn. Proceeding back in procession to the various schools, the youths carried banners of different colours to render the spectacle more imposing, upon which were various inscriptions and devices, dictated by the missionaries. One of these bore an inscription which we think characteristic. Besides the white doves and olive branches which were the general devices, on a banner of white native cloth was impressed, in large letters of scarlet dye, the single word 'Hosanna!'

Such meetings as these were certainly well calculated to affect the imaginations, and interest the feelings of an amiably disposed people, who had only lately emerged from a state of barbarism and idolatry. At another meeting, which was held in 1824,—with picturesque effect, upon a peninsula or pier jutting into the sea,—six hundred children assembled and were feasted by their parents.

CHAPTER XIII.

Improvement of the Islanders in the Art of Building. Schools and Chapels in Huahine and Raiatea. Royal Mission Chapel in Tahiti. Mr. Ellis's Voyage to Tahiti and Eimeo.

Among the improvements of this people in the arts and in civilization, which were so rapidly introduced into the Georgian islands, after the general reception of Christianity, none were more remarkable than those connected with the erection of private and public buildings.

Instead of the miserable open-sided sheds which, in many districts, contrasted painfully with the rich and noble scenery of nature, and with which many of the indolent inhabitants were contented, before they became acquainted with European comforts; they now began every where to copy the more elegant and convenient buildings of the missionaries.

Frames of new houses were every where set up, formed upon principles of carpentry more scientific than had ever before been introduced. Boarded sides and floors were added to the more durable roofings; and glass windows began to be in request in the new houses of the chiefs. The art of burning lime was also speedily learned by the natives, and the handsome little dwellings which studded the beach at the bottom of the bay, or peeped forth from the hill-sides or the groves, being plastered with lime, assumed a gay and agreeable appearance.

But it was in the newly erected schools and chapels of the different islands that the natives showed both their ambition and their taste. In Huahine a chapel was commenced in 1819, and finished the following year, which was an hundred feet long, sixty wide, and thirty high in the centre of the roof. The walls were plastered within and without, the windows closed with sliding shutters, and the doors were hung with iron hinges of native workmanship.

The pulpit was supported by six pillars of a beautiful satin-like wood, which grows on the island. The pannels were of the rich yellow wood of the bread-fruit tree, and the frame work of a fine wood of a dark chestnut colour, contrasting well with the pannels of yellow. The stairs, reading desk, and communion table, of a deep amber-coloured bread-fruit, showed specimens of native workmanship, such as the islanders might well be proud of; for the building had been completed by the people.

Meantime, in Raiatea, a building for a similar purpose had been erected, which, as well as the former, was finished in the month of April, 1820; and, on being opened, was found to contain two thousand four hundred people within its walls. Round the pulpit were the seats for the chiefs of the island; and in the evenings, the missionaries having contrived to erect a rude species of chandeliers, they were, to the admiration of the natives, lighted up for public worship.

The frames of these chandeliers were made of a light but tough wood suspended from the roof, and the lamps which were of the common sort, were made of the half shell of a cocoa-nut, with oil and wick. The natives, when they first entered the chapel, and beheld it lighted up in this brilliant manner, never having before seen so many lamps burning together, started with astonishment and admiration.

But the greatest wonder of this sort, was the enormous building erected by King Pomare in Tahiti, which was called the Royal Mission Chapel of Papaoa. 'It is probable,' says Mr. Ellis, 'that, considering the Tahitians as a Christian people, he had some desire to emulate the conduct of Solomon in building a temple, as well as surpassing in knowledge the kings and chieftains of the islands.'

In May, 1819, when the encampment of the natives who had flocked to attend the anniversary of the missionary society, extended along the shore a distance of four miles, this great chapel was opened for worship. Seven thousand people entered the chapel, and, divided into three congregations of above two thousand each, were ministered unto by three different preachers at the same time.

We now proceed to give a brief account of one of the last of Mr. Ellis's voyages among these islands, which was to Tahiti, and this also affords an opportunity for some notice of the state of the mission in that island, to which a few of the missionaries had returned, as before stated, after the general change, and to second the brilliant prospects which had then been opened by the conversion of the king.

Among the changes which had occurred in the circumstances and policy of these islands, schemes of trade had been entertained by Pomare. Into the details of these it belongs not to our plan to enter, but they called Mr. Ellis from his labours in Huahine, to attend a consultation of missionaries, and make one of a deputation appointed to wait upon his majesty, at his residence near the old station of the missionaries at Matavai.

His voyage in his small boat was rapid and agreeable; for, having advanced about an hundred miles in twenty hours, at midnight he heard the roaring of the surf over the coral reefs, as it dashed against the steep rocks of the harbour of Taloo in Eimeo; and in an hour after, shooting swiftly into the deep bay, they made the shore.

Late as it was, Mr. Ellis proceeded up the valley, to the residence of one of the missiona-

A NIGHT ON THE BEACH.

Page 182.

ries, whom he roused from his sleep, and where he was accommodated for the remainder of the night. His companions on the voyage having in the meantime spread the sails of the boat upon poles on the beach, to serve as a tent, kindled a fire, and went to rest.

Next day, it being quite calm at sea, Mr. Ellis determined on not continuing his voyage till evening; and this gave him an opportunity to address a congregation of the natives. In the evening, at eight o'clock, they again put to sea; and having cleared the harbour, and entered the wide Pacific, he began to make arrangements for performing his night voyage in safety.

Knowing the disposition of the natives to become drowsy, and slacken in their watching towards the morning, he determined to take a short nap himself first, in order that he might be the better able to watch while the others were in danger of giving way to sleep. Having placed a trusty man at the helm, he accordingly lay down on the seat at the stern, and soon fell asleep.

The easy motion of the boat had so well

rocked him in his unanxious slumbers, that when he awoke, not a sound was to be heard around him, nor could he for an instant collect his senses to think where he was. What was his consternation, on looking up, to see the broad day-light, the man at the helm fast asleep, and every one of the other islanders also in sound repose, in different parts of the boat.

Such a situation of men in an open boat, on the bosom of the Pacific, was as strange as it might have been dangerous. But they were yet within sight of land, being about half way between the island they had left and Tahiti; the lofty mountains of which began now to appear, in the clear light of the morning sun.

Mr. Ellis awoke his companions, who looked round them and rubbed their eyes in ludicrous confusion, scarcely believing the evidence of their senses, as they saw day-light, and were told that the whole ship's company had been buried in sleep. The sea, however, was extremely calm and smooth, and taking to their oars, a few hours' hard rowing after so sound a nap, brought them to a place called Burder's point in the island of Tahiti.

Landing at this point, Mr. Ellis soon came to the missionary station, where he, and the native chiefs associated with him in the deputation, were gladly received. Here they found marks of the same improvement, so rapidly advancing in all these islands. Besides the comfortable plastered houses, and the flourising gardens, a public burying-ground, situated on the borders of the settlement, and surrounded by a neat wall, bore evidence of the progress towards the refined sentiments of civilization.

A convenient school-house was also erected; and a compact chapel, built near the ruins of an ancient marai, or temple of idols, was not only supplied with seats and pulpited within, with neatness and good taste, but was likewise fitted up with a gallery,—the first that had been seen in the Georgian islands.

Leaving this station, and rowing along the coast, Mr. Ellis came to another, near a place called Wilkes's harbour, and not far from which the queen and her sister were then residing. The chiefs, who accompanied our missionary, having gone to the residence of that lady, he,

12

after a short interview with her, went to the settlement of his brethren.

The principal missionary established here was Mr. Crook, whom we have more than once had occasion to mention, as having been originally left by the Duff in Tongatabu. Mr. Crook was living with his family in an agreeable and elevated situation, on the brow of a hill, which he had called Mount Hope, and which, being on the extremity of a low ridge, that swelled into the interior of the island, commanded an extensive and delightful prospect.

Here our missionary spent the Sunday, having preached to an attentive congregation of five hundred persons; and on the following day, again meeting with the chiefs, he proceeded to the well known district of Matavai, where Pomare, the king, now resided. The business of deputation having been partly accomplished, Mr. Ellis took up his abode with the veteran missionary, Mr. Nott.

With him he consulted respecting the framing of those laws and public institutions, which were afterwards established among these islands, to the everlasting honour of missionary effort. At length, on the fourth of May, he took his leave.

Having sailed speedily back to Eimeo, his voyage home to Huahine, the scene of his own immediate labours, was again in the night. Parting from the romantic scenery of Eimeo, shortly after they had witnessed the enchanting effects of the short twilight upon the mountains, as they rowed slowly on, the shadows gathered around them, and they found themselves on the solemn stillness of a calm night on the Pacific Ocean.

The night was moonless, but not dark. It was passed by the voyagers in reflection, and occasional conversation. Their little vessel soon came in sight of Huahine, and on the Sabbath morning, they landed again in Tane harbour, and gave thanks to that Providence which had restored them to their friends and families in safety.

CHAPTER XIV.

Visit of the Vincennes to the South Sea. Condition of the islanders. Turnpike. Mausoleum of Pomare. Sunday at Matavai Bay. Raiatea. Meeting of the chiefs. Address of the native chieftain. Festival. Visit from the Queen. Her letter to the President of the United States.

The limits of our volume will prevent the notice of many interesting voyages to the South Sea. The only remaining writer, whose work we shall have occasion to consult, is Mr. Stewart, a chaplain in the navy of the United States, and formerly engaged actively in missionary enterprises. He visited the islands described in the foregoing pages, in the public ship Vincennes, during the years 1829, and 1830, and has given the result of his observations during that period in two very interesting volumes.

Mr. Stewart describes in a very gratifying manner the improvements in personal comfort and moral feeling, since the introduction of Christianity among these islanders. The spacious white chapels, the parish schools, the pleasant dwellings of the missionaries, and the neat habitations of the natives, scattered among the orange groves and graceful palm-trees of these luxurious islands, present a picture of interest and beauty hardly to be surpassed by any scene in the world.

The ship in which Mr. Stewart sailed anchored in Matavai Bay, at Tahiti, within about a mile of the beach, and nearly opposite the high red bank called 'One Tree Hill.' The visitors were favourably received by the natives, and by the European gentlemen who were resident there, for purposes of trade, or of imparting religious instruction to the natives. Among those of the former class was Mr. Bicknall, who was the owner of a considerable plantation, not far from Matavai Bay.

His house was a new frame building, boarded at the sides and end, with a roof of thatch in the native style ; the wooden part being neatly painted in cream color, with doors, Venetian blinds, and a covered veranda in green. Within, every thing was neat and elegant ; while horses and mules, herds of cattle and flocks of goats in the adjoining fields, testified to the prosperity of the worthy planters. Here also was a sugar mill with the boilers, and a ware house filled with fine sugar and molasses.

In riding about to pay visits to the different missionaries, Mr. Stewart travelled on a turnpike, which has been constructed almost to the length of an hundred miles, nearly the whole circumference of the island. It was built principally by convicts, who had been condemned to labour for various violations of the laws.

It is broad and well gravelled, reaching in almost direct lines from point to point of the coast, and is provided with narrow wooden bridges, over the streams and water courses, that flow from the mountains to the sea. 'Thickly embowered with luxuriant groves of various trees, skirted here and there, with the humble but comfortable habitations of the islanders, opening occasionally upon a bright glade or extensive meadow land, with fine views of the mountains on one side, and the ocean on the other, it is, in many places, beautiful as a drive in the pleasure ground of an American mansion, or the park of a gentleman in England.'

The mausoleum of the kings Pomare I. and II. is a white plastered house, in a large enclosure, embowered in the deepest shades of the groves. Near it, a section of the great chapel, erected on the king's conversion to Christianity, is still standing, and is used as a school house. The original length of this building, it will be recollected, was more than seven hundred feet, and its width more than fifty.

Mr. Stewart describes a Sunday at the settlement at Matavai Bay, in so interesting a manner, that his account is worthy of being copied in all its minute details. What reflections must it excite in a thoughtful mind, while reading this description, to compare the present condition of the Tahitians, with their former melancholy situation. But a few years ago, a gloomy idolatry and degrading superstition, joined with customs of the most brutal and disgusting character, had sunk them almost to the level of brutes. Their altars flowed with the blood of human victims, and fathers destroyed their infants with their own hands!

On the occasion to which Mr. Stewart alludes, the morning of the Sabbath was opened with a meeting for the purposes of prayer. It was attended by large numbers of the natives. About nine o'clock, a Sunday school was held in a neat building, erected for that purpose in the neighbourhood of the chapel. Here were assembled about one hundred and fifty youths, of both sexes, from the age of three or four to that of seventeen years. In the midst of them were several middle aged men, engaged in the duties of instruction, while others walked about the room, to observe and correct the deportment of the numerous scholars. Many of the parents and friends of the children were also present as spectators.

The exercises commenced with an examination in the catechism, in which the answers were generally ready and accurate. This was followed by a recitation from the Bible. A hymn was then sung, in which all joined, and the whole was closed with an appropriate prayer. While engaged in prayer, the sound of a bell was heard from a neighboring grove, calling to church; and shortly after, the scholars in a quiet procession, walking two by two, were on their way to the temple of God.

Crowds of islanders were at the same time observed, gathering from every direction, and following the well leveled gravel walks to the neat place of worship. They were all clad in modest and respectable garments, principally white, and some of foreign manufacture. In their whole aspect they were serious and dignified, and preserved an air becoming a christian people. Almost every individual carried a copy of a portion of the scriptures, printed in the native language, and a volume of sacred songs.

The number of worshippers amounted to about four hundred: including most of the residents in that neighborhood. Their conduct was throughout as decorous, as that of any Christian assembly in Europe or America. 'A single glance around,' says Mr. Stewart, 'was sufficient to convince the most sceptical observer of the success and benefit of missions to the heathen.'

To his intelligent mind, it was perfectly clear, that they can be rescued from the rudeness of their savage condition, can be taught reading and writing, good manners and good morals, and be raised to the full enjoyment of all the blessings that Christianity promises to man.

When the Vincennes had left Matavai Bay, and arrived by the shore of Raiatea, her officers paid a visit of ceremony to several of the native dignitaries. Among these were the queen of Tahiti, the dowager, her mother, an aunt holding the office of regent, with a train of inferior chieftains, all of whom had arrived the day before from Tahaa. The interview took place in the house of king Tamatoa. All present were dressed in European costume, more or less complete in the articles constituting a full suit.

When the conference was ended, the king of Raiatea and his queen, attended by the dowager and regent of Tahiti, retired to one of the inner apartments. Shortly after they returned, bearing beautiful presents of mats and native cloth, which they laid at the feet of the Captain. At the same time, the street door was thrown open, and the steward of the queen's household stepped in, and pointing at a large quantity of fruits and provisions, of various kinds, presented them with much pomp and ceremony to the Captain, as a gift from his mistress to the officers of the Vincennes.

Just before taking leave of the island, the officers were invited to attend a monthly meeting of the secondary chiefs of the island, held for the discussion of matters of general interest. On this occasion, several of the chiefs, in suitable and animated addresses, declared the great pleasure they received from the visit of a ship from the government of the United States, and the happiness afforded by the kind and conciliating deportment of the American officers and marines towards the natives.

In reply, the Captain of the Vincennes assured them that the kindest feeling existed in regard to themselves and their people. He expressed his interest in the improvements which religious instruction had introduced in their condition. He encouraged them to unwearied attention, both in themselves and in their children, to the means of knowledge with which they were favoured, and to the enactment and observation of salutary laws. To these remarks one of the most distinguished chieftains made the following reply :

'Chieftain and Friend,

'This is my speech to you. Great has been the joy of our hearts since your arrival among us, because of the kindness of your object in this visit. We greatly rejoiced on the Sabbath day, for your presence with us in worshipping the Lord : and in bringing your band of beautiful music to unite with us in praise. This made our hearts very glad.

'You are now advising us, and strengthening us in our small and feeble government—you are encouraging us in the acquisition of letters, and in the formation of laws : this is good. Should any thing prevent the benefit of this encouragement in the affairs of our government, still may your great nation countenance and promote the work of God among us Gentiles; and patronize our teachers in doing their good work.

'Health and salvation to yourself, chieftain, and to all the nobles and christians of America!'

After some refreshments at the mission house, the Americans returned to their ship, much pleased and gratified with the incidents of the morning. At the request of the queen, the band was sent on shore in the afternoon, and a kind of concert was given in the chapel, that was very numerously attended. As the day had been a sort of festival, an exhibition of rockets and fire-works was displayed from the ship in the evening, much to the delight and astonishment of the natives.

On the morning of departure, the queen of Tahiti and her party called on board the Vincennes, for the purpose of despatching a letter to the President of the United States. Of this interesting document, the following is a translation:

Raiatea, September 26, 1829.

'President,

'In consequence of your kindness I write a letter to you. You sent a man-of-war formerly to our land, commanded by Captain Jones; he treated us with great kindness. You have now sent another man-of-war, commanded by Captain Finch; his kindness to us has also been great: we are highly pleased with his visit. I now write to you to express my gratitude; also to inform you of our present state.

'I am a female—the first queen of Tahiti—Queen Pomaré I. is my name. I am daughter to Pomaré II. When he died the government devolved on my little brother—he died, the government then became mine. I am young and inexperienced.

'We have cast away the worship of idols, and have embraced the worship of our common Lord. In the year 1814 we embraced Christianity.

'We have missionaries on the island, who are diligent in teaching us that which will promote our welfare. Some have been with us upwards of thirty years.

'We have laws by which we are governed. I cannot send you a copy, I being on a visit to my grandfather at Raiatea.

'Tahiti and Eimeo are the largest islands in my government. We have not many people—perhaps ten thousand.

'There is not much property at my island—arrowroot and cocoa-nut oil are the principal. We have abundance of food, and excellent harbours for ships: many American vessels call at Tahiti—tell them to continue to call, and we will treat them well.

'All kinds of cotton cloth are in demand here for barter—white, printed, blue—shawls, ribbons, axes, are all good property to bring, to procure refreshments.

'We have a new flag given us by Captain Lawes, of the Satellite, British man-of-war; will you kindly acknowledge it in traversing the seas, and in visiting you, as yours is by us—should that be the case at a distant period.

'Captain Finch has made myself, and mother, and aunt, with others, some handsome presents in your name, for which receive my gratitude.

We are always glad to see American vessels at Tahiti. Continue to sail your vessels without suspicion. Our harbours are good and our refreshments abundant.

'Prosperity attend you, President of the United States of America,—may your good government be of long duration.

Queen Pomaré I.'

THE END.

Zeitfracht Medien GmbH
Ferdinand-Jühlke-Straße 7
99095 Erfurt, Deutschland
produktsicherheit@kolibri360.de